MW01234742

Carl Elton Cook holds degrees from two reputable American universities. From 1991 to 2008, he served as a contributing editor for *20th Century Guitar Magazine.* Currently, he is involved with music and video production as the songwriter/guitarist with the rock band SpamRisk. He lives a quiet pet-free life at his home in Ohio.

For Chic and for Pic.

Carl Elton Cook

# THE MAYFLOWER PROJECT

AUSTIN MACAULEY PUBLISHERS™

LONDON • CAMBRIDGE • NEW YORK • SHARJAH

**Ordering Information**
Quantity sales: Special discounts are available on quantity purchases by corporations, associations, and others. For details, contact the publisher at the address below.

**Publisher's Cataloging-in-Publication data**
Cook, Carl Elton
The Mayflower Project

ISBN 9781638297536 (Paperback)
ISBN 9781638297543 (Hardback)
ISBN 9781638297550 (ePub e-book)

Library of Congress Control Number: 2023901914

www.austinmacauley.com/us

First Published 2023
Austin Macauley Publishers LLC
40 Wall Street
33rd Floor, Suite 3302
New York, NY 10005 USA

mail-usa@austinmacauley.com
+1 (646) 5125767

Although I could never acknowledge all the fine people that made *The Mayflower Project* possible, there are a special few that warrant my additional gratitude.

Firstly, this book would have never happened without the influence of Carl Sagan. One evening around 1991, I was watching a particular episode of Cosmos that dealt with the subject of deep space travel. Sagan explained that it would be virtually impossible to travel far enough or fast enough to ever reach much further than our planetary neighbors. I went to bed that evening pondering the science of space travel. Like one of Einstein's mind experiments, I came to the realization that the only way to accomplish this feat was to rely on the participation of generations of people. Years later, I recognized that there was a story to be told. *The Mayflower Project* was born.

Looking back further, I recall the profound influence of my high school English teacher, Pamela B. Williams, as well as my college English professor, Ashraf M. Syed. Both taught me that one's best effort will never be easy and to always try harder and dig a little deeper. In addition, they instilled an understanding of the power of the written word. Lesson learned.

*The Mayflower Project* went through countless rewrites and edits. A thanks is due to my friend, the late Lee Secrest, for his assistance with editing and proofreading the book. Lastly, I must thank Amber Lynn Montevideo. She worked tirelessly to edit the manuscript in addition to completing the formatting necessary for a salable presentation. Additionally, she submitted the final manuscript to Austin Macauley for publication.
So, here it is. Thanks, one and all.

Carl Elton Cook
February 2022

# Part One: Prelude

# Chapter 1

It seemed like an eternity but was only a small portion thereof, maybe fifteen minutes tops, since Colonel David Stratford heard the engineer depart the workstation situated outside his office door. He listened to his steps as they faded into an ever-softening echo, eventually substituted by the soft 60 Hz. hum of the antiquated overhead lighting. He had been lost in abstract thoughts, sitting at his large mahogany desk, as rays of sunlight spread like an oriental fan across the floor, furtively climbing the opposite wall.

When Stratford came to inspect his office this last time for any personal effects that might have been overlooked, it was probably Wooster, or was it Woofter? Although he had never known for sure what the man's name was, it had to be him, as he was the only other person on the second floor. Plus, earlier last week he glanced at the office reassignment chart, and Woofter was to be the new occupant of his office.

Woofter had been with the World Space Organization for a relatively short time and was the chief designer of the horticultural section. In fact, he was there just long enough to get the systems in place and was not under Stratford's immediate influence. In the last few months, Colonel Stratford made it a point to avoid getting involved with anyone new. Besides, the guy appeared to be a typical PhD Geek, a fairly common type around there.

He had already spoken his farewells, brief and austere though they were, to most of his staff yesterday. He was by nature a man of economy: few words, little possessions, and hardly any deep attachments to anyone. Stratford had always carried minimal baggage through life, first as an Air Force officer, then as a NASA space program volunteer. So, this Woofter was just one more WSO flunkie he wouldn't have to look at again. Stratford's wife Lydia was a nurse/nutritionist and had briefly trained in Woofter's section. She described him as a bit full of himself; intense and uncompromising in his principles. Probably, not unlike Stratford himself. Strange…Stratford was a little surprised when he, Mr. W., hadn't dropped by to discuss the office transition or the Mayflower Project itself. Perhaps, it was fallout from Dr. Hardin's blanket policy instructing the WSO resident staff to minimize any sense of finality or feeling of separation the flight officers were bound to experience in the last days before departure by discreetly avoiding the topic whenever possible. But still, not even a cursory 'good luck'?

Stratford had made arrangements for the removal of the last of his personal effects yesterday, but it was his style to imagine they would fail to make a thorough and complete job of it. He was forced to revise his opinion slightly, as a quick search of his desk revealed that nothing had been left behind. He knew that ultimately, these artifacts would end up in some museum; probably Wright-Patterson, possibly even the Smithsonian. The realization of this fact made him feel rather like a foreign body in his own office. Why, he wondered? As the Mayflower's commanding officer, he'd been given this chance at historical immortality, but it was kind of like dying.

The room suddenly felt askew and rather unfamiliar. The clean patches on the wall indicated where the numerous framed mementos and testaments to his life's achievements had formerly and formally, resided. He knew that later that evening the janitorial service would scrub it antiseptically, so by Monday morning, Woofter would inherit a spotless cubicle, donated from the Colonel's own space-time continuum. *Kind of like dying*, he thought.

Stratford looked through the window. On the tarmac below, his eyes accepted a sharply protracted image of the space shuttle Olympia, which was being readied for tomorrow morning's flight. Its metallic surfaces had taken on a luminous quality in the late summer evenings' half-light. He shuddered involuntarily as his nervous system desperately tried to expel the image. He tried unsuccessfully to disconnect from it, even as it drew him closer. Like it or not, tomorrow morning he would be at the controls, and all the wearisome training he had undergone at the WSO would evolve into an entirely different reality.

# Chapter 2

Only Stratford, his wife, and four other husband-wife crew members remained for the final rendezvous flight to the Mayflower, which had been taking on personnel systematically for the month. Earlier that year, the Colonel had completed two training exercises aboard the ship, so he was already quite familiar with the craft. Specifically, he was profoundly impressed by its majestic expression of technologically advanced engineering and old-fashioned chutzpah. It was huge, more accurately, gargantuan and surely the ego equivalent of mankind sculpted into form. The ship had been launched in pieces over the last several years and assembled in an orbit just beyond the Earth's outer atmosphere, which was an impressive feat in itself. Not only was it grand in scale, but also purpose.

Power was supplied by three separate nuclear reactors, two of which drove turbines to give the craft impetus, while the other powered the life support systems. Water predictably cooled the reactor cores in slow orbit, while the icy vacuum of space could be harnessed at speed to cool the entire three tier system.

Originally, the Mayflower Project was a NASA brainchild, and Colonel Stratford was one of only a handful of former NASA boys who stayed on after the United States governments' transference of titles and properties to the private sector, when the WSO was born. Money changes everything – including the Mayflower Project. After NASA sold out, countries, companies, and even individuals invested in the WSO, thus helping to expand the scientists' original intent but at a dilution of central control. Despite the drawbacks, though, the scientific community and the WSO were free to expand the frontiers of space exploration, thus evolving the entire fabric of the Mayflower's intended purpose. Contrary to US government principles, they could now recruit the finest minds available.

During NASA's brief three-year tenure as the Mayflower's birth parent, the craft was intended to be the long-promised sky lab they had been predicting since the 1960s. It took the altogether more advanced WSO engineers to find a superior utility and purpose for the Mayflower. One capable of harnessing its capabilities. In fact, after the WSO took over, things changed dramatically. For one thing, the media had deliberately been misled initially about the Project's expansion of purpose. Not misinformed, but actually misled. The public relations puppets made no effort to correct any false preconceptions the media may have had. Yes, they freely acknowledged it was a scientific space laboratory, and yes, prior to its development it was impossible to traverse vast distances. Indeed, such distances were only imagined by most and only seen by those with privileged access to powerful and expensive telescopes.

Stratford had always loved the name: Mayflower. What a beautifully ironic, poetic, and cosmically perfect name. Others loved it, too. The President of the United States described it at the White House ceremonies after the true details of its intended destination came out, as a ship equaled only in its drama of purpose by the original Pilgrim's crossing of the Atlantic Ocean in the first Mayflower. Stratford thought at the time that although true enough the President's comparison was pathetically understated. The President then went on to describe the Colonel and his crew as 'Pilgrims for a new tomorrow,' or some such nonsense. He didn't see himself as a Pilgrim. No way. The Pilgrims' little excursion might better be compared to a leisurely and languid walk in the park. Even the NASA expedition to Mars he had led some seven years before was a mere bird walk in comparison to the Mayflower Project. No, Stratford knew what the big picture was, even if the politicians didn't. He was, as a matter of training, an Air Force officer, but by inclination, he was also a scientist. Science was dispassionate. Science was also objective, meticulous, and impartial. From the overall historical scheme of events, there was Erikson, Columbus, the Wright Brothers, Yeager, Armstrong – maybe even Lindbergh. But none of them could touch this.

Stratford stretched his arms fully extended behind his head, stifling a yawn. He got up from the desk and walked toward the window for a better view of the swarm of activity that had begun around the Olympia. He forced his left hand through the grimy blinds at roughly eye level, and then retracted it to wipe the gray residue from his fingers. Placing his hand back again, he forced the blinds apart and could see that ground crew technicians had entered the cordoned-off area to begin their final inspection and preparations for the next morning's departure. Many separate arcs of light began tracing a path up and down the Olympia's sleek form as so many human insects tested, perhaps tasted, its worthiness. However, for all its sophisticated grandeur, it was still just a glorified jet plane.

Realistically, he knew that as the commanding officer of the Mayflower, he would be more akin to a systems manager, an administrator, like Mr. Danning, his grade school principal. Ultimately, this self-image was somehow acceptable to him, because in the final analysis, the power would reside with him – and power, he knew, was what it is all about. Mr. Danning sure as hell knew it. He was probably six years old when Mr. Danning made the announcement over the school's public address system that the entire school – in an orderly fashion by grades one through six – would meet in assembly to watch John Glenn's historic splashdown after their historic walk on the moon. How confident we were as a nation back then! We seemed assured of success in everything we did. However, Vietnam eroded some of the Yankee cocksureness and was probably the first chink of many in the armor of this great nation.

In addition, our advanced sense of scientific self-worth was irreparably damaged when the Challenger exploded upon take off. After that, elementary principals were much less inclined to parade their young charges into gymnasiums across the country to watch any other potential NASA fiascos. Stratford recalled that at least one unfortunate principal was actually sued by some demented parent and her parasitic lawyer after the Challenger tragedy. Demanding millions, each attempted to site "irreparable trauma" incurred as a direct result of watching the disaster.

After this, Stratford had jokingly postulated that there should be a class action lawsuit brought against colleges and universities for matriculating too many lawyers and mostly defective ones at that. It pretty much summed up, in Stratford's mind, what had gone wrong with the entire American system. In a word, it was driven by greed. People pursued money as if they were going to live for a thousand years and even after death, needed the cash. We had become a nation where stupidity and failure were held as virtues, while honesty and worthy yet middle class efforts were punished. It was no wonder he was glad, no, relieved to be getting out.

Stratford glanced at his wristwatch. It was nearly 6:30, and he remembered Lydia would be expecting him for dinner. He looked back at his watch, and turning his wrist to and fro, he smiled in spite of himself. Some eighteen years ago, his parents had given him the watch as a graduation present, a congratulatory commemorative that would mark his completion of Officer's Training School. *It probably should be left behind*, he thought, with his other personal possessions: i.e., relics. Left behind for another generation or two to revere, covet, or admire. After all, given the destination, time was a meaningless commodity. Besides, who the hell needed a watch? This reminded him of the scene in *Easy Rider* where the character played by Peter Fonda, Wyatt, threw his watch down in defiance of social restraints and went off with Billy to discover America, only to find his vision of America didn't exist.

Perhaps Stratford's version of the dream didn't exist anymore either, and that's why he welcomed the Mayflower Project and the exodus that loomed before him. Time, and the constraints it represented were just one more societal construct he hoped to escape. With that, he carefully unfastened the leather strap and contemplated leaving the watch on top of his desk. Would it be properly cared for or catalogued if he did that? Hell, it was probably more likely to be stolen by someone in the janitorial service hoping to cash in on its instant value. No…on second thought…tomorrow morning he would give it to the properties' supervisor who would place it with the other pieces of his life. He dropped the watch in his coat pocket, turned from the window, and walked to the doorway, stepping into the workstation area beyond. He disobeyed an impulse to look back over his shoulder and instead strode quickly to the elevator. He waited impatiently for the doors to open. Hit the button marked "1" before pressing the "close door" button out of habit.

Damn it! He had left the office light on.

The remaining Earth-bound members of the Mayflower expedition, including David and Lydia Stratford, were housed in lavish quarters, deep in an underground facility beneath the WSO building. The entire Mayflower team consisted of one hundred and ten candidates, made up of fifty-five couples. They had spent the last month of their training in these suites. As each designated team readied themselves for departure, the next group took up residence in the vacated quarters. This system-in-rotation had proved necessary to minimize the complexities encountered with learning to adapt to life aboard the Mayflower. Using Air Force terminology, each group of ten people was referred to as a "flight"; all other flights had been shuttled aboard the Mayflower, and Stratford's was the last one. As the commanding officer, Stratford had spent a few days of instruction with the earlier flights to familiarize himself with the duties of each department. This was considered necessary to develop a sense of loyalty and camaraderie for the man who was to be their assigned, as opposed to chosen, leader. This world in microcosm would function much like any social system found on Earth. It had been theorized that inevitably loyalties and factions could occur, which could undermine the mission if not carefully planned for.

The first flight installed aboard the ship consisted of engineering/maintenance specialists – those responsible for overseeing the critical functions of the craft's power supply and life support systems. Subsequent flights were shuttled aboard the Olympia, upon completion of their instruction. The logistics of the entire operation, such as the choosing, testing, and training of personnel was so far beyond normal comprehension that the design of the master plan had largely been carried out by large, mainframe computers. Adding to the already wearisome burden placed upon the candidates, each person had to specialize in at least one other discipline in addition to their primary assignment. Ingeniously, this allowed the WSO to ensure an absolute minimum number of appointees while ensuring backup personnel.

Colonel Stratford's degree was in physics, but he also held an advanced degree in mechanical engineering. Hence, there were several critical positions he could fill temporarily if needed. Should he become incapacitated and unable to fulfill his duties as the Mayflower's Captain, the ship's command would pass to the next ranking first officer and if so, needed a second officer. The Mayflower's constitution was simplicity itself, and it was drafted with provisions to elect officers from the rank and file if the need should arise or if something befell all three officers. It looked like they had thought of everything.

# Chapter 3

Colonel Stratford disembarked from the elevator. As he approached the door to his suite, he noticed a food service orderly had noisily turned down the hallway, pushing a stainless-steel cart ahead of him. The man wore a black and gold plastic name tag that read "Scott Ripley," and beneath it, "World Space Organization." In addition, clipped to the lapel of his freshly laundered white jacket was his WSO plastic I.D. card. This particular orderly was familiar to the Colonel, and he stopped short of his destination to exchange greetings. As it happened, they shared destinations and continued together.

"Hi ya, Colonel, I thought that was you," Scott smiled, as he reached for Stratford's extended hand. "I have your order here – yours and Mrs. Stratford's." Scott looked down at the order sheet taped to the edge of the cart. "There's a rack of lamb, Maine lobster, baked potatoes, salad, chocolate mousse cake, a pot of coffee, and for later," Scott said. He then snapped his finger against the shiny ice bucket on the second shelf, producing a pleasant chime…"a bottle of Asti."

The Colonel guessed what Scott was trying to subtly address while pointedly avoiding the topic: a bottle of wine to toast your farewells. "Sounds perfect, Scott, thanks. I was just upstairs in my office…" the Colonel's voice trailed off. "Well – anyway, follow me."

As they walked the short distance along the dimly lit corridor toward his suite, Stratford felt at a loss for something to say. "Did my wife turn in our breakfast order to the kitchen yet?" he asked, continuing after the orderly indicated that he was unsure. "In that case, let me check if it's still here and give it to you, if you don't mind. All I really want is something light…just black coffee, and some Quaker oats with brown sugar. Let me see about her."

"I haven't spoken to her personally, sir, but I assume if she did call the kitchen, it won't be any problem changing it," Scott answered, as they approached Stratford's suite.

The Colonel was reaching in his coat pocket. "Wrong pocket," he muttered to himself, as he fingered the watch he placed there earlier. Finding his keys, he simultaneously pushed the service buzzer next to the doorbell button to alert Lydia that their meal had arrived. Unlocking the door, he pushed ahead first to hold it open for the orderly.

"Thank you, Colonel; if you'll just hold it a second, I can manage."

Stratford had already grabbed the front of the cart and began pulling it toward him. "Got it, Scott," Stratford said cheerily, implying it was not necessary for him to proceed beyond the entranceway, but the orderly failed to connect with his meaning. He already tried keeping this encounter brief when he asked about the breakfast order. He figured Scott would leave hastily if there was no need to wait for the order. No matter. Stratford began walking backward, pulling the serving cart as the orderly pushed. The rusty wheels created a hollow rolling sound followed by a muffled brushing when they encountered the mauve carpeting. Upon reaching its final resting spot beside the dinner table, Stratford was more than prepared to rid himself of the overly-jubilant and utterly-disingenuous waiter.

Meanwhile, Lydia had been in the kitchen arranging the necessary dinnerware paused and put aside her task to greet her husband. "David," she called. "Why did you ring the service bell? Oh…hi, Scott; that explains it," she added. "I didn't see you at first."

Respectfully, Scott nodded his salutations as Lydia joined them. "Evening," he added softly.

"Well, it's like this, honey," Stratford said in a put-on, drunken manner. "I had a few too many, and Scott here," he indicated the orderly and the cart behind him, "drove me home."

"Oh sure, out drinking at the club and raising hell we were, Mrs. Stratford." Scott picked up the Colonel's lead. "We did manage to save a bottle for your dinner." He reached under the cart and grinned slyly as he pulled the ice bucket and its emerald bottle out and placed it on the table.

David became suddenly uncomfortable with the banality of this exchange, and sought to shift it to something less jovial. "Scottie has your lobster here, Lydia – what did you say it was, Scott? Maine lobster?" David addressed each in turn.

"Yes, sir, whole Maine lobster."

"Wonderful," Lydia smiled. "I love lobster."

19

Scott made a face. "Better you than me, Mrs. Stratford."

"Oh, you don't like it, Scott?" Lydia asked.

"No, I don't do the lobster. I kinda don't favor foods that require an assist from Black and Decker," to which the Stratford's laughed heartily. "Not to mention, I think I heard somewhere once that lobsters are related to spiders, and I don't like their cousins, either."

Stratford had decided upon lamb for his "last good meal for the road," as he had described it that morning when Lydia asked him what he preferred for dinner that evening. Not surprisingly, nearly all flight members had chosen fairly exotic fare for their last supper before their departure to the Mayflower. Although the frozen cache stored on the craft was quite vast and varied, it also was finite. Good nutrition would not prove to be of major concern; however, because in addition to the frozen foods, they would also have fresh fruits and vegetables. A substantial horticultural section was aboard, and through the use of large overhead artificial sunlight generators, many familiar garden fares could be raised by both advanced hydroponic techniques and conventional organic means. As a source of sweet golden honey and to serve as natural pollinators, a bee colony was housed aboard ship as well. For fresh sources of needed protein, several species of fish – trout, walleye, and catfish would be bred and raised in a specially designed aquarium. Additional sources of critical dietary staples required large lockers where freeze-dried fruits such as oranges, grapes, and apricots were kept. It gave new meaning to the term 'trail mix,' as Stratford said when he observed the lockers. For other dietary requirements not found in large quantities in the foods raised aboard, many would be synthesized by the well-equipped pharmacy. Certainly, it would not be like "Mom used to make," they knew; yet, it wouldn't be all Tang and beef jerky, either.

Realizing his presence might constitute an intrusion, Scott cleared his throat in preparation for a convenient, painless departure. "Well, Colonel Stratford, Mrs. Stratford, I hope you both enjoy your…your supper…" he paused. "It's always been a pleasure serving you both." Scott cleared his throat again. "I know everyone in the kitchen is wishing you the best…" His voice trailed off as the clutched feeling in his throat now turned into an emotional "frog" of epic proportions. He wasn't finding any useful words that expressed good-bye without actually saying it, so he stopped trying, and stood mutely fingering the handle of the dinner cart.

Lydia was the first to bridge the awkward moment. "Scottie, that's very sweet of you. Thank you ever so much. You've always been so helpful. The Colonel and I have always appreciated your efforts."

Stratford was grateful the emotional exchange had been quarterbacked by his wife. "That's true, Scott," he began, then tried to reintroduce the levity he crushed earlier. "And thanks for driving me home, too."

Scott laughed and infectiously, the Stratford's joined in, relieving them of any further sentimental obligations on their part. The Colonel picked up the bottle of Asti Spumante in an attempt to indicate that dinner was waiting. Scott followed the cue, and as he wheeled his cart toward the door, Stratford addressed him one last time. "Oh Scott, keep working on that college degree – you'll get through it just fine." The orderly had once explained to the Colonel that he had higher aspirations than remaining in the food service department at the WSO, and that he attended college part-time, pursuing a degree in Business Administration. It flattered him to know that the Colonel had obviously taken a genuine interest in his life's endeavors, recalling this small, but important detail. Scott nodded in the affirmative repeatedly, as a small boy might while being lectured in some obvious tasks.

"Lydia," Stratford turned to his wife as the thought occurred to him. "I already gave Scott my breakfast order, but what are you having? Did you call the kitchen yet?"

Lydia gave an obligatory "no" in response to her husband, and then addressed the orderly. "Scottie, please, I'll just have some buttered wheat toast, orange juice, and black coffee."

"You bet, Mrs. Stratford."

Scott was halfway through the door at this last exchange and gave a comical half wave, half salute with his free hand. Finally, the door snapped firmly shut, leaving the Stratford's alone.

Lydia looked with a smile toward the table. "Well, let's see what we can do about this," indicating the table's bounty. She raised her eyebrows inquisitively at her husband when he did not immediately respond. Instead, he walked around the edge of the table, closing the physical gap between himself and his wife for the first time that evening and grasped her waist tightly with both hands.

"Not so fast, my dear, always thinking of food, aren't you?"

"No," she caressed the back of his neck as she playfully bit him lightly on the chin. "But I am so famished, Colonel Stratford, sir," her voice lilted musically. "I'd just as soon have you if you don't turn me loose."

"I think you'd find me tough, little lady," Colonel Stratford joked.

"Oh, I don't think you're all that tough," Lydia mused.

"But I am. Tough and loaded with cholesterol," he replied.

"Is that good cholesterol, or bad cholesterol?" she inquired, eyes wide in mock innocence.

"You know what they say, don't you?" he inquired.

"No, tell me," Lydia playfully answered.

"No chews are good chews," Stratford said, then broke into a bottled-up laugh.

"David," Lydia let out an exaggerated groan. "You have to be kidding with that." She maneuvered herself laterally, and Stratford gave up his grip, acknowledging his defeat with a shrug.

Such an exchange was typical of the Stratford's private moments, when they revealed a side to each other that was exclusive to their marriage. Their public masks were rigid and dignified as befitted their professional roles, while in each other's presence, they might relax into child-like word play and frivolities. These vignettes demonstrated a much deeper, central truth: they were unfalteringly devoted to each other.

Dinner was a predictably quiet affair. They discussed minor aspects of their day. Stratford related the visit to his office, while Lydia had logged her personal affects for removal, pointedly avoiding tomorrow's departure for the time being. With their banquet completed, Stratford had opened the well-chilled bottle of Asti, and they restfully sunk into the soft cushions of the living area's davenport. Lydia had switched on the TV-more as a distraction than as a means of entertainment. The movie guide announced the George Stevens's classic, *Giant*, and although they tried to follow the story, they became momentarily entranced in the movie's flickering illuminations. There was a lot to say to each other…in this most significant of evenings…and they were merely biding time. Dr. Keith Hardin, head of the Psychological division of the WSO, had knowingly sent along the bottle of sparkling wine.

At that moment, James Dean filled the big screen, pacing off his postage stamp chunk of Texas real estate. With a self-confidence that was borne more in naiveté as opposed to any legitimate birthright, Jet Rink, his character, climbed the old water tower, imagining the unfolding of possibilities as he surveyed his domain. The scene engendered a silent reverie in Stratford. He sat his wine glass down and pulled Lydia close. She hit the sound on the remote, lowering the volume just as the music began to swell accentuating the mood Rink's ambitions.

"Lydia," Stratford began tentatively. "I've always felt it was my destiny to do some great thing; something important and lasting. Until this came along," which Lydia interpreted 'this' to mean the Mayflower Project. "I had resigned myself to the fact that my Air Force career and the Mars expedition were supposed to be enough." Stratford stopped to weigh his words and emotions before continuing, while Lydia reached out tenderly to take his hand. He turned slightly to look her in the eye. "But they aren't enough." He repeated himself. "They're not nearly enough."

After this, he turned back toward the movie and fell silent. Picking up the remote he absent-mindedly flipped the channel several times, settling for a moment on what was obviously some high-fashion event. One of those reality shows, perhaps. Both he and Lydia looked on in amusement, Lydia allowing her husband to organize his thoughts. "I wonder," he offered finally. "Maybe the pursuit of success is the same drive to accumulate wealth. Do you think so? A kind of wealth for the soul, maybe?" He sought condemnation or redemption from Lydia, trusting her enough to accept what she would say. "Do you understand me – or am I completely crazy?"

Lydia's answer reassured him. "No, I don't think you're crazy. I've always known you had a potential for greatness. I feel the same way, David, but not for exactly the same reasons. I've never wanted to achieve any great thing, but I would like to be part of some great purpose. Perhaps, the Mayflower Project is the answer for both of us."

"Perhaps? Hmmm. That's not particularly reassuring, my dear," Stratford teased. "It might only mean that you're as crazy as I am."

"If that's true, then I promise I won't tell anyone the truth about us if you don't," Lydia vowed in mock seriousness.

The Stratford's returned their attention back to the TV. Several young models were sashaying their way down a runway and toward the screen. These beautiful, leggy models all shared well-rehearsed, couldn't-care-less expressions while their breasts flopped under sheer, anonymous dressings positioning themselves in novel and revealing ways. It occurred to Stratford that these young women were supposed to somehow be civilization's highest expression of "femininity." A pinnacle that all other women should aspire to be and all men covet. The next model to appear was a blonde of especially generous endowment. She had obviously brought Western advancements in beauty aids to bear in improving what nature had been frugal with. 'Bleached blanket bimbos,' Stratford always called them. He reached for the remote without bothering to consult with Lydia, and the screen went dark. He'd had enough. The hour was late – making him think about his watch again. This was the last night. He hadn't really noticed, but they had drunk the whole bottle of wine – and it must have performed the function Dr. Hardin knew it would.

"Lydia," Stratford began. "I want to tell you. I am so grateful for you; through everything I've ever done, you've always believed in me. Now, it's this, the Mayflower Project." He turned toward her and rested his hand on her arm. "No second guesses now. What differentiates this from the Mars expedition…is that we'll accomplish it together."

"I really believe, David," Lydia answered slowly, choosing her words with care, "this is the accomplishment…the big achievement you've always wanted."

Stratford laid his head back on the davenport and inhaled deeply. Was she right? It hardly mattered, either way, because there would be no more chances after this. "Yeah, but I wonder," he agreed with reservation, "maybe it's a little too big."

While Stratford understood his personal drives well enough, he was, however, unacquainted with deeper motivations, the ones that resided in his subconscious, his bones, blood…his DNA. Lasting immortality eclipses mere fame, being grounded in primeval urges as old as mankind himself. Ever since the first proto-humans climbed a taller tree or scaled a higher peak in a vain attempt to penetrate the evening's veil and touch the stars, the physical limitations that held him back were broached in agonizingly slow degrees. These barriers were at last shattered by ever more sophisticated technology – personified by the Mayflower. The Faustian pact man had made with science placed a formerly unobtainable paradise within reach of his shaking, outstretched hand – gained at an incalculable price:

*We are stardust*
*We are golden*
*We are billion-year-old carbon*
*And we've got to get ourselves*
*Back to the garden*


Dr. Keith Hardin had listened patiently to this, the tenth caller that evening. All were futile attempts to speak to the Stratford's prior to their departure in the morning. As the director of the Psychological Division of the World Space Organization, it had been Hardin's edict that all calls intended for the Stratford's, or any of the other deportee's, be forwarded to him. They already learned from other flights how emotionally distressing these calls could be, so he decided to make it a matter of policy to screen all of the calls.

"…I assure you, sir, I do not have the authority to override my own rule where this matter is concerned…Yes, I know what I told you before…I agree; I should have been clearer in my meaning, but as it stands, even I can't place a call to the Stratford's and get through…No, the only possibility would be if they happened to call me…I'd say, to be honest, slim to none…I am very sorry to disappoint you, sir, but I will tell them in the morning anything you'd like…He'd be pleased…Yes, I'm writing it down…I won't forget; I'll give them this note…Thank you, yourself, for your understanding…Yes…Thank you, Mr. President…Good night."

# Chapter 4

The television anchors, radio commentators and newspaper reporters, along with their support technicians had been swarming the WSO's facility since early dawn. Like so many vultures lured by the scent of ripe carrion, the WSO security guards repelled their advances with a passive authority and little else. The struggled outcome was being decided in favor of the officers as no weaknesses had been breached and the buildings' doors remained sealed. During their long wait for newsworthy personalities to appear, the media had been resigned to making bland observations or even interviewing each other – barely serving the thirsts of the public at large for coverage of the event. However, there would be no official comments from the WSO, and media contact with this last departing crew, unlike previous flights, was strictly prohibited. Free access to any of the Mayflower's members had been curtailed by Dr. Hardin after the circumstances surrounding the last Olympia shuttle flight were revealed, and he wasn't about to let it happen again.

Having completed their extensive pre-flight briefing, the ten departing members at last entered the reception area. Their appearance set the media beast into an agitated frenzy of noise and motion – its activity strangely coordinated as if a commensal colony of sea anemones. When Stratford and party at last appeared, dressed in the visually striking gold and black uniforms, the entire body pressed closer to the glass, moving to and fro, arms flailing, seeking any advantage to overwhelm the guards and claim its prey.

The crew was accompanied by five aides and some top-ranking WSO officials; however, the chairman, Robert Hendrickson, and Dr. Hardin were not among them. The aides were occupied with attending to minor details for their charges – handling the effects and flight materials which they would remove and store aboard the Olympia. No one else had been permitted in the building for their departure, including any relatives of the members. This particular policy might have appeared overly restrictive, but it was believed necessary to preserve a healthy outlook for the crew. One parameter that had been central to the exhaustive process of selecting Mayflower volunteers was the issue about family. Without exception, none of the couples chosen could have any children, whether fully grown or otherwise. In Colonel Stratford's case, he had no parents and no siblings, which was all the better. Lydia did have a younger sister she was close with; David only had Lydia.

Stratford appeared disturbed. He had been surveying the reception room's far perimeters, taking in the furor and excitement generated by this event. The egocentric side to his personality would have gladly bathed in the glorious moment, while his detached, analytical side regarded the media with considerable suspicion and resentment. For one, he disagreed with Hardin's policy change of sequestering them from the press, believing contact would not have impaired his ability to separate himself from his Earth-bound brethren. On the contrary, he couldn't think of any good reason to stay, anyway.

Momentarily, he noticed that Dr. Hardin had arrived and was engaged in conversation within a small entourage that included Robert Hendrickson, as well as the WSO spokeswoman, Ruth Kaslow. The identities of the other two members of the party did not immediately register with Stratford, then it flashed suddenly: it was Michael Woofter, of all people, and the woman must be his wife. Stranger still, the couple was dressed in WSO flight suits. Dr. Hardin had noticed Stratford's inquiring look, and turning toward him, crooked a finger and beckoned for him to join them. As he approached, the entire group displayed a friendly, expectant look, while Stratford observed that Hardin's face alternately expressed pleasure and mild apprehension. "Colonel David Stratford, I'd like to present Mr. Michael Woofter and Mrs. Jane Woofter," Hardin said as he grandly served as master of ceremonies. The two men clasped hands, while the Colonel only nodded respectfully and mouthed a silent greeting to Jane Woofter.

Woofter spoke first. "It's a real pleasure, David. I've seen you around the WSO, and I'm sorry we've never had the chance to speak before this. It will be an honor to serve with you."

"Will you please excuse us for a minute," Hardin broke in. "Excuse me, Michael," and he encircled Stratford's shoulders conspiratorially with his arm and led him a short distance away. Stratford had bristled slightly at Woofter's informality. His irritation escaped through his eyes, which Hardin noticed.

Granted, "Colonel" was a now outdated title he earned as an Air Force Officer; assuming the stewardship of the Mayflower, he would be known as "Captain." Few people called him David.

"It's like this," Hardin began, offering his explanation about the Woofter's presence close to Stratford's ear. Like a coach. "Three mornings ago, we received a message at the Command Center from the Mayflower that Richard Bentz and his wife had decided they could not participate in the Project, and their immediate removal was requested." Hardin paused, allowing the impact of his statement to sink in before continuing. "Unfortunately, there wasn't time, or a convenient point to discuss this with you. On the one hand, it would have made little difference even if we had brought the matter to you, because this is the way it is."

Stratford remained silent during Hardin's shocking revelation. He had easily anticipated the outcome, but waited to hear him out.

"At first, we thought it wise to keep our options open as there was a chance they might change their minds." Hardin said, then shook his head emphatically. "But it's like Hendrickson said: 'We don't want them out there if they aren't one hundred and ten percent with us,' and I agree." He pointed with his free hand to indicate the Woofters. "We immediately put them on standby alert, being the first-choice alternates, and it was decided only yesterday they would indeed replace the Bentz's, which didn't give them much notice to put their affairs in order."

"Did they give a reason?" Stratford asked, meaning the Bentz's.

"Apparently, it was a mutual decision on their part. I didn't speak to them directly, but I understand they described it as a 'moral crisis,' whatever the hell that's supposed to mean."

"Well, Doctor," Stratford stood back, and Hardin's arm dropped to his side. "I don't know Woofter, but I am aware of his work, and his reputation as a scientist, so I have no qualms about the substitution. Hell, he was the one who designed the garden complex on the Mayflower. Maybe he'll prove to be an even better choice than Bentz was. Besides, I gather this is just a formality. You're telling me about this, not asking…right?"

Hardin broke into an embarrassed smile. Stratford might be the Captain of the Mayflower, but he wasn't in charge of the WSO, nor, for that matter, was Dr. Hardin. "Well anyway," he said briskly. "That's how it is. We're both just hired hands."

# Chapter 5

Woofter's presence on the second floor of the building last night, and his apparent reticence to speak to Stratford made perfect sense now that he understood the dynamics of what had happened. So, there would be a new horticulturalist. "What are the plans for getting the Bentz's out?" it occurred to Stratford suddenly, fearing the logistics could delay the Mayflower's departure.

"I understand the auxiliary shuttle Romulus is serviceable, and is being prepared," Hardin said as he looked at his watch. Stratford again remembered his own watch – he must remember to give it to a WSO aide. "If it isn't, it should be ready within the next twenty-four hours. After you've boarded, and the Olympia is secured, they'll plot the new coordinates for your rendezvous with the Romulus."

"How long are we talking for all of this?"

"The best estimate we have is it will only delay the Mayflower's departure by one or two hours at the most."

"Well…whatever it takes. It's too bad about the Bentz's," Stratford offered. "I had gotten to know Richard fairly well during some training exercises, and he always seemed like a conscientious man."

"Yes, I had felt they were both a good fit for the Project, but you can never talk about these things," Hardin said, unsure how much he wanted to or even should say. "That's one reason we decided to keep the media away from your group, David," and both men glanced at the still writhing presence beyond the glass walls. "I'm not going to belabor the point, but I understand that Bentz…well, never mind. We don't want them, as Hendrickson said, if they don't want us, right? The Woofter's asked to be a part of it – and besides, it was Michael who developed a lot of the advanced horticultural methods being used on the Mayflower."

"Yes, I was aware of that."

"He had worked on it originally as a private consultant before we brought him in to oversee the design of the garden complex. Shortly after getting involved, they asked to be considered as alternates. Anyway, don't worry about Woofter, David – he's an absolute boy wonder. In a way, this change could prove to be for the better."

"I hope you're right," David replied. "Lydia worked with him during some of her training. She described him as a bit arrogant: single-minded and arrogant."

Hardin laughed and grasped Stratford's arm. "Well, I hope you two don't clash out there, because sometimes I might say that describes you."

Stratford took Hardin's comment in stride, giving him back a tight-lipped smile. "No argument from me, Doctor. But if he's that good, I'll be glad he's aboard…" Then he grew defensive. "Maybe he'd say the same for me."

"Well…anyway," then Hardin remembered the note he'd written down last night from the President, and reached inside his coat pocket and extracted the folded communication. "I almost forgot, David. This is from the President; I spoke to him last night, and he asked me to write this down – don't bother to read it now," he reached out and stopped Stratford. "Put it away and look at it later." His face broke out in a big, toothy smile. "Save it; you may want to give it to your grandkids someday."

# Chapter 6

It was Hardin's think tank. Stratford had preferred calling it a "shrink tank" that created the tests and ultimately chose which applicant couples were suited for the Project. To the best of Stratford's knowledge, there was no instance where their recommendations were reversed by the WSO board. As far as he was concerned, Hardin was still testing them; probing and gathering data, and collating findings.

One unpredictable variable that Hardin, nor the other designers of the Mayflower Project gave little thought to, was the darker psychology of those who signed on. Surprisingly, when word of the enterprise was quietly disseminated first through the scientific community and later the world at large, the WSO received many more applications than could be effectively dealt with. A screening agency was set up to weed out the obviously maladjusted applicants. It had not occurred to Hardin when the search began how many misfit Earthlings there were out there. Resumes and telegrams, phone calls and e-mails poured into the WSO building from every walk of life and every corner of the globe.

On a superficial level, it was reassuring to reflect on how many fearless explorers were ready to make such extreme sacrifices. Yet, Hardin's band of shrinks knew the score about the demons in these peoples' heads, and they were reluctant to examine the facts too closely. There were sealed reports rumored to exist that Hardin "misplaced" and never showed the WSO board. The truth was that anyone at the outset who actually wanted to participate in the Mayflower Project should have been immediately excluded. But on the other hand, who would you sign on if you excluded the volunteers – the people who didn't want to go? It was a real conundrum and a Catch-22, to be sure.

The candidates were shown the standard array of Rorschach ink blots; they took polygraph tests, submitted to hypnosis, and had their personalities inventoried pretty thoroughly with the MMPI. They had private interviews, group counseling and in general, the conclusions were always the same, no matter how the results were purposely skewed. This was not a representative sampling of Homo sapiens. With a collective shrug of the shoulders, a crew was finally chosen that was the least screwed-up of all the applicant couples tested, and so the Project went forward.

# Chapter 7

The shuttle Olympia was being held in standby for its departure. The engines were at low idle, forming passive clouds that rolled from its six exhaust ports and spilled onto the tarmac. The cool dawn air was saturated with mist, while the rising sun illuminated the space craft through a fog formed by both machine and nature. Meanwhile, the ship's passengers were ensconced inside, awaiting clearance from the Command Center tower to begin this first leg (and shortest phase) of the exodus that lay before them.

To the disappointment of the assembled media, these last remaining members of the Project issued no final statements. Once the sealed door of the WSO building was opened, they were quickly ushered onto an airport bus escorted by armed guards a mile to where the Olympia had been towed down the runway. Hendrickson authorized this extra security because of the recent increase in threats received at the WSO. In private, he bitterly referred to the lunatics sending them as the 'abolitionists.' It was only a week ago that one such complainant nearly succeeded in demonstrating his extreme displeasure with the Mayflower Project. A single, white 35-year-old male nonentity who lived with his mother tried leaving ('absent-mindedly,' his lawyer later informed the court) an armed pipe bomb on the grounds of the WSO. Thankfully, the plain brown package was sniffed out by one of the bomb squad German Shepherds, a champion ironically named "Ted" where it had been "forgotten" under a bench right outside the headquarters' front doors, the plaintiff's rights to free expression notwithstanding.

After this Mayflower team was safely installed aboard the shuttle, Hendrickson and the other WSO officials retreated to the underground facility to watch their departure in relative safety on the closed-circuit system. It was then that WSO spokeswoman Ruth Kaslow stood for open questioning outside the building. Her curt replies of 'no comment,' or 'our position has remained consistent on that' wore thin quickly with her inquisitors as well as the great body of humanity watching the drama unfold on their televisions.

"Captain, all personnel are secured and ready." Steve Lester, second officer and radio operator, responded over his helmet's internal microphone to Stratford's question.

"Roger then, Steve, request clearance for takeoff."

Michael and Jane Woofter were ensconced in the very rear of the shuttle. In Stratford's opinion, they were practically stowaways. In the cockpit to Stratford's right sat Albert Breck, co-pilot, and the Mayflower's first officer. Breck's wife, Patricia was lateral to, and just behind Steve Lester in the cramped area directly below the pilot and co-pilot. Thomas Reddie, navigator, sat with his wife, Pamela, a nurse, in the first seats directly behind the pilot and co-pilot. Lydia Stratford was paired with Diane Lester, a medical technician, and they were behind the Reddie's. The last two passengers were Ramon da Silva, a computer systems programmer and his wife Maria, a surgical nurse, who were located forward to the Woofters.

"We have word, Captain; we are now cleared for takeoff. We are cleared for takeoff," Lester's voice reverberated in everyone's helmets and in their bones. Momentarily, his voice cracked again. "Dr. Hardin extends his best wishes, as does the entire mission control room," then paused as he listened. "He's saying that Mr. Hendrickson spoke with the President a few moments ago who wishes us…I quote…'success, happiness and I hope you break a leg.'" This last statement elicited a sizeable laugh from the entire ships' occupants.

"Tell mission control we copy and a great big 'thank you' from all of us," Stratford said, and then he turned to his co-pilot, giving a thumbs up to which he received the same gesture in return. "Hold tight, people," Stratford advised loudly, as everyone braced for the upheaval. Breck pressed a series of control panel switches that sent an adrenaline rush of fuel to the engines, which responded with a deafening rise in decibels as the craft leaped and shuddered forward.

Michael Woofter reacted to the acceleration by physically leaning into the very Hand of Technology as it placed its palm over the front of his body and tried squeezing him through the seat. Jane observed his struggle and reached over and gripped his arm. "Are you alright, Michael?" she shouted. Woofter looked at her and nodded. Sensations rushed through him that transmuted into emotions as his subjective experience blurred. He looked out the thick-paned portal window to his left and desperately tried to reconnect to something reassuring, something Earthly; a tree, a building, anything. The only result was he disconnected even further, as colors became separated from their form and disappeared into whirlpools of shade as the Olympia went faster. The shuttle's acceleration climaxed as its wheels separated their grip from the runway, and it hurled suddenly airborne. As it gained altitude, the morning sky outside its windows darkened by ever subtler degrees, becoming at last a clear midnight blue. Stratford expertly leveled the craft, cruising at a comfortable MACH 25 once the Earth's outer atmosphere was penetrated. At Thomas Reddie's direction, he then banked into a long sweeping arc, and all felt the centrifugal force acting on the Olympia. Progressively, the Earth began to recede into the near horizon, as the ship made good its escape. Woofter finally could relax, as his vital functions returned to normal.

"Ladies and gentleman, I'm happy to report we're still in one piece," Stratford announced. "Mr. Lester reports from the Command Center a round of congratulations." Everyone cheered and clapped, muffled though the sound was from their heavy gloves. "Next stop – Mother Mayflower."

Among its more impressive attributes, the Olympia's ability to affect a horizontal takeoff made the craft infinitely safer and more versatile than any of its predecessors, being able to land on and then take off from an orbiting spaceship, this being the last necessary advancement that made the Mayflower Project possible.

# Chapter 8

Although they had little time to fully assimilate their decision to go, both Michael and Jane felt blessed in being given this opportunity to be included as members of the Project. Michael was a Harvard-educated plant physiologist, author, and horticulturalist who had earned a substantial reputation in his field. When he was all of thirty-two years old, Michael had chaired the Botany Department for three years at Kentucky State College and was a highly respected academician – a rare privilege for one so young. Having grown bored quickly with university life, he then retired to his private estate where he conducted research in developing strains of vegetables for greater size and nutritional yield. Fearful of the unpredictable impact of modern agribusiness in the overall ecology, he counseled that size of vegetables was of no inherently greater value than nutritional content.

Given the limited type of gardening that could be conducted on the Mayflower, his work was of great interest to the designers of the Project from the very outset. His landmark book, *How to Feed the World*, had a profound influence not only in purely scientific circles but also for the casual backyard amateur. It had only been as recent as a few months ago that he was chosen to lead the research team at the WSO – formerly headed by Richard Bentz. Bentz's work had been no less regarded than Woofter's, although not as well known. He had been responsible for the adoption of certain exotic fare; i.e., Eastern or Oriental plants such as pomelo and loquat for the Mayflower's table. It was in the area of unfamiliar plants of great nutritional value that his knowledge remained unsurpassed.

Thomas Reddie's voice broke the silence in the cockpit. "Colonel… er…Captain, we have the coordinates in place for rendezvous. We expect to be in sight of the Mayflower within minutes."

"Copy, Tom," Breck responded for the Captain.

"Request a plot for our approach and speed," Stratford instructed Breck. "And let us know when he has the numbers in place."

"Aye, sir. Mr. Reddie, please advise us of the new coordinates once you have them."

"Roger, copy. Working on them now."

While he had been absorbed with putting the Olympia safely into space, Stratford had forgotten the two surprise passengers, and thought now to inquire as to Michael's state of mind. Using the complex, yet easily manipulated switching system of the ship's communications, it was possible to conduct one or more private conversations, or in any other possible combination. Stratford chose to keep this courtesy call open for the entire ship's benefit. "By the way, I'm sorry if we've neglected you back there, Woofter. How are you getting along with all of this so far?"

"Fine Stratford, fine," the gardener declared. Everyone, including the Captain, correctly guessed the reason for Woofter's gentle jab at Stratford: he was not intimidated by anyone. It's better to get it straight now, he figured. "The takeoff was a bit bumpy but exciting. It kinda of reminded me of the old Blue Streak roller coaster at Conneaut Lake Park when I was a kid."

"Well, we're glad we could show you a good time."

"There is one other thing, though," Michael added mysteriously.

"What's that?"

"Jane and I were wondering," and he nudged his wife knowingly. "When will cocktails be served, and is there a movie on this flight?"

Virtually everyone laughed in appreciation of the gardener's dry wit…even Captain David S. Stratford.

Albert Breck picked up the ball. "Well, there's two-year old vintage grape Kool-Aid for you, Michael, and the movie we offer tonight is a double feature: *Attack of the Killer Tomatoes*, and its popular sequel, *Killer Tomatoes in Orbit*."

"Very funny. Thank you, Mr. Breck." Michael practically shouted to be heard above the raucous outbreak of laughter, taking the obvious reference to his professional interests in good humor.

# Chapter 9

At length, the crew and passengers became absorbed in their assigned tasks or private contemplations, interrupted only by need or inclination. For the Woofter's, these last few harrowing days had hardly been enough to absorb the impact of their decision to replace the Bentz's. Certainly, the Project required sacrifice…many of which might be considered unconscionable. For one thing, it demanded complete separation from family, friends, and the associated pleasures of being a part of the Earth community. They were giving up so much for so little personal gain. As for the gardener and his wife, they were leaving their beloved estate in the rolling Kentucky countryside – the renovated centuries-old farmhouse and the large complex of laboratories/greenhouses Michael had built for his research. In a hastily arranged meeting between their lawyers, the Woofter's had turned their properties over to Kentucky State College to be used as their new agricultural research facility. Other than some trifling personal effects that were distributed to their respective families, all other financial assets were placed in a trust to continue the work, which Michael Woofter had devoted his life.

The Olympia's passengers were suddenly shaken by a series of violent jolts, which were accompanied by a change in pitch of the engines to a lower, throaty roar.

"Sorry about the turbulence, people," Stratford's disembodied voice floated barely above the din. "Everything's fine. That was just a 'downshift' you felt." His next statement was lost entirely as the craft shook again; seemingly, it was attempting to go backward. Breck began a litany of statistics that were intermittently audible amidst the groaning protestations of the engines. "We have MACH 24…checking functions…MACH 24…that's MACH 23.75…"

It was Steve Lester's voice that broke through next with a simple pronouncement that would forever remain unchanged in the collective consciousness of each expatriate: "Ladies and gentlemen, we have before us, the Mayflower." Those words, like a child's laboriously rehearsed first communion, but somehow holier, a first kiss, perhaps, remained as indelible as the visually stark presence of the Mayflower itself. Its architects had birthed its monstrous blueprint with special care from the onset, and its dimensions were awe-inspiring. It was 3.8 miles in length; its height equaled an eight-story building at the tail section where the garden complex was housed, and it was 1.7 miles wide. Overall, it was best described as wedge-shaped from front to rear, while a gull-like arc shaped the midsection from port to starboard, giving it an appearance of a bird in flight, or even a manta ray. The Mayflower's life support systems were no less impressive than its size, making it a completely self-contained and self-sustaining environment. Beneath the skin of the inner bulkheads, there was a mammoth network of air purification filters that traversed the ship for literally thousands of miles, designed to remove all manner of contaminants, particularly carbon dioxide. While the garden complexes' extensive array of plant life would provide some oxygen, the Mayflower's designers knew it would be of no more importance than a supplemental source. The air purification facility coupled a series of chemical reactions between the captured $CO_2$ and a volatile mixture of reactive acids and manganese to generate oxygen as its by-product. Likewise, fresh water was of no concern for the travelers, as nearly 1600 gallons could be produced artificially every twenty-four hours using a polarized electric field in the presence of solid and liquid wastes from the garden's fertilizer production. Equally astounding, the Earth-like gravitational conditions were derived from the fusion-driven reactors, which drove the electromagnetic turbines and produced a satisfactory artificial gravity.

Communications had by this time been established with the Mayflower, so that many dispatches were being sent and received in turn. As the shuttle continued to decelerate, Stratford began a series of ever shortening elliptical orbits in the approach to Mother Mayflower.

"Roger, Olympia, the landing deck is elevating. We estimate the deck will be fully extended in T minus four minutes. You may land at your discretion after T minus four minutes."

All the passengers were awed by the sheer spectacle as the ship's back opened along its length revealing a-mile-long fissure. An angled platform of intensely contrasting yellow-orange was slowly rising to receive the space shuttle. As Michael Woofter watched, he suddenly recalled the melody to a David Bowie song, *Ground Control to Major Tom*.

Michael laughed to himself. "Hey, Ziggy, how's this for a space oddity!"

Being scientifically grounded, Woofter well knew that songs or movies with themes of space travel might play as high drama or at the very least good entertainment, but they were very bad science. Strangely, few people questioned the *Star Wars* version of fanciful physics and actually believed space travel to other galaxies was possible. The same could be said of the believers in UFO's. All manner of miracles were attributed to aliens, from the building of the pyramids to the creation of crop circles in the English countryside. As if interplanetary beings would traverse endless space to smash stalks of corn into indecipherable geometric patterns, only to leave upon completion of the task. Medieval lunatics would have attributed such proceedings to witches, while the atomic age versions blamed aliens. The scientific reality was, however, that the distances between stars were too great. You simply could not travel fast enough and far enough to actually arrive anywhere worth going. Once the purveyors of fantasy were forced to accept the hard science, they began to devise ways to go farther rather than faster. This was the key that made the Mayflower Project more than a notion and much more than science fiction.

Even when the Mayflower Project was first conceived, astrophysicists had a hell of a time coming up with a destination. Proxima Centauri was only 4.2 light years away, and it was a known "G" star. One whose characteristics were similar to our own sun, yet there is only a single planet in that binary system with habitable conditions. However, this planet is both tidally locked and subject to frequent solar flares make it virtually uninhabitable for humans. After the launching of the Newton telescope, the astro boys finally came up with a worthy destination: the star was called Tau Ceti, and it was in the Constellation Cetus, or the "Whale." They discovered two planets in orbit around Tau Ceti – which they named Earth 2.0 and Earth 3.0. Both were believed to be ideal candidates for human colonization. There was only one small technical glitch, however, to the whole plan: Tau Ceti was 11.9 light years away. A few simple calculations revealed that even once the Mayflower achieved its full velocity of 240,000 miles per hour after a year or so of traveling in frictionless space – it would still take 33,201 years to get there. What the WSO psychologists needed was a team of altruistic volunteers who would place the greater cause and concerns of the Project ahead of their own – antisocial tendencies aside. It was upon this crucial ideal that the success of the exodus rested. It would require unswerving loyalty, and a commitment to scientific ideals.

More to the point, it would require devoted couples to fulfill this most magnificent of human endeavors. To transport his kind 11.9 light years to colonize another planet also required one other supreme and admittedly morally ambiguous sacrifice. They would raise their children during the span of their lives, instructing them in the breadth of their skills while instilling in them the same determination of purpose as they held to complete the Project. Then the children shall dispense this knowledge unto their children and their children too. The triumph of man's technology was personified by the Mayflower, while the expression of his indomitable will was the children. It was this partnering that would make the Project possible, as well as, renewable resources and an inexhaustible power supply. Renewable crews made it all possible; moral ambiguities be damned. It was the only way.

# Chapter 10

The landing lights on the now fully extended landing deck were illuminated and the shuttle had reached a sufficiently diminished velocity so that Stratford felt confident enough after a few practice maneuvers to land. Having made a third pass, he announced his intention to crew and passengers. "I think I have the right moves, so hold on people, we're taking it in." After reaching the furthest point in his elliptical orbit, he negotiated the Olympia into a gentle sweep, nose up and bore down toward the mother ship. Stratford directed Breck to cut the throttle back during the descent to one-third power, causing the engines to produce a low whistle. Contact with the landing deck was imminent and was announced by a sudden, springy impact as the wheels rebounded violently, and the heavy deck cables grabbed the undercarriage. It seemed to Woofter, contrasting with the takeoff, that now his body would squeeze through the shoulder harness slicing him into neat packets of gelatin, perhaps. The cables snapped tightly, and the remaining kinetic energy was dissipated.

"Is everyone okay? Any problems, anybody?" Stratford asked, but no one responded. "Steve, if you will please inform the Command Center we are down and still in one piece." It was then that a murmur of appreciation arose among the other Olympians as they realized the glad truth; they had made it.

Stratford threw back his harness, and while he and Breck clumsily shook gloved hands, he addressed the passengers again. "Lydia, everyone...please just stay in your seats. Remember, we have to wait until the deck retracts and the ground crew can fill the landing area with heated atmosphere before we can disembark. It's a little cold out there, and these are not sub-zero suits."

Everyone was conscious of movement as they settled back to watch through the portals as the landing aperture closed, decreasing the icy blackness overhead. Once sealed, the rushing sound of oxygen enveloped in thick veils of eerily glowing clouds became evident. Occasional glimpses revealed the infrared heating elements on the bulkheads surrounding the shuttle's perimeter which imparted a red-orange glow to the mist; once the area had filled, the clouds dissipated.

"Captain, it looks like our welcoming committee has arrived," Tom Reddie observed. Indeed, four gold and black attired figures had entered the landing area through a heavy door some yards away with two other WSO-clad members trailing behind.

"Maybe so, Tom," Steve Lester tentatively agreed. "Could be space troopers here to hand our Captain a space ticket for exceeding the speed limit. What do you think?"

"Parking lot attendants," Woofter said inaudibly, to no one in particular.

The procession of six separated as they approached the Olympia. The four in front disappeared from sight, while the other two, a man and a woman, walked directly toward the shuttle's hatch door.

"Officers, secure systems and everybody prepare to disembark," Stratford instructed. "I think we can take these pickle jars off our heads now too."

With much relief, the others happily obeyed, freeing themselves from their restraints and their helmets. The passengers stood and stretched reflexively and began peeling off their flight suits, gladly leaving them piled on the seats. Both Stratford and Breck abandoned the cockpit and entered the passenger compartment. Lydia Stratford took her husband's embrace, quick and undemonstrative as it was, while the other officers engaged in similar reunions with their wives.

Three soft raps sounded from what seemed to be the lower hull. Tom Reddie was closest to the door, and he sprang the seal electronically. Then, he pushed it outward with a pronounced snap. "Let's see if there's any intelligent life here," he joked.

"There will be now if there wasn't any before," Breck returned.

The four ground crew personnel reappeared, wheeling a portable staircase into position. The weary travelers began to exit the Olympia with deliberate and careful steps, almost like sailors finding their bearings on land. Lydia Stratford, followed by the Captain, descended last. Stratford recognized the couple at the bottom of the steps. It was John and Christine Morrison, the Mayflower's husband and wife entertainment officers/historians. John had been a minor Hollywood celebrity whose best-remembered role was a network TV remake of *The African Queen*. Morrison was the gin-guzzling hero Charlie

Allnut. His wife, Christine, had been a fairly popular Canadian actress, who met with some success in international film productions. They both had been early enthusiasts for the Mayflower Project, being among the very first volunteers chosen.

"Colonel…ah, pardon me…I guess it's Captain Stratford now," John Morrison said brightly, "a demotion and promotion all in one." He clasped Lydia Stratford's hands, "Mrs. Stratford, so glad to have you both aboard." Morrison turned to address the others who had gathered to await the dispersal of their personal items. "Everyone, if I may have your attention for a moment. Some of you may wish to go immediately to your cabins to rest, but if any of you desire anything at all, let me or Christine know. Dear," he said to his wife, "please see to it that Mrs. Stratford gets settled in; I need to discuss a few things with the Captain."

Stratford looked aside at Lydia, and placing his hand behind her elbow, guided her gently, as if confirming Morrison's instructions. "I won't be any longer than necessary, Lyddie, and I'll join you at our cabin," he said, his voice ending in a note of uncertainty.

Lydia smiled. I understand. I'll wait there." After gathering their belongings from the shuttle's storage compartment, she allowed herself to be accompanied to the exit with Christine Morrison. The other officers and their wives departed as well.

While disembarking, the receiving area had become awash with a myriad of activities as the ground crew made preparations to remove the Olympia to dry storage. The technicians, Stratford knew, would summarily remove any unspent fuel, and the life support system would be drained clean as well. Afterward, the lines would be pumped full of non-corrosive drying agents. Because the Olympia would be out of service for a considerable time, it was imperative to carefully preserve its delicate structures, like a mummy. The shuttle could again be revived and brought forth when needed to fulfill the colonization of Earth 2. It was the vital link that began and would complete the Project, given that it was equally impossible to land the Mayflower as it would have been to launch it.

# Chapter 11

John Morrison's voice only carried slightly over the sounds of dry docking of the Olympia. "Colonel, I have to fill you in on some of the recent developments with Richard Bentz," he shouted, then looked toward the landing area's operations office. "We can't talk here…let's step in there," and proceeded to lead the way. It was only after stepping through the doorway they noticed the room was occupied by two technicians who were overseeing the mothballing of the shuttle, but neither of them took any particular notice of the Captain or Morrison. "I don't know how much Hardin told you, or at what part of the story he left off," Morrison resumed the conversation. "I can tell you this…in the last few hours since you left, it got way out of hand."

"I was only told about it just before takeoff," Stratford admitted. "Frankly, there's damn little of it that made sense."

"Well, yes," Morrison nodded in agreement. "I have to agree, it doesn't make sense to me, either. But it gets worse."

Stratford was sufficiently intrigued now. "Tell me what else happened."

"I'm not sure how to begin."

"Pick a spot, John, try the beginning."

"Okay, but I have to tell you this first. I was told by Hendrickson himself that this is to be kept as quiet as possible."

"Right, right," Stratford said testily. "I understand. Just tell me what it's about."

Morrison pulled in a deep breath to fortify his resolve as much to give weight to what he had to say. "A few hours ago, Bentz tried to sabotage the life support nuclear reactor."

Stratford was visibly stunned, and shook his head in amazement. "You've got to be kidding," he said loudly, and one of the technicians glanced at Stratford. He regained his composure before continuing. "Did he do any irreparable damage?"

"Not really. There are so many fail safes. He only managed to destroy a water temperature control panel, and they were able to replace it. Believe it or not, he used a garden hoe to smash the thing to bits."

The image of Richard Bentz wielding a hoe against the Mayflower provoked an involuntary chuckle in the Captain, founded in the absurd visual of it. Morrison laughed too. It was sort of funny, despite the circumstance.

"Anyway, once we were able to subdue him, Dr. Phen placed him under sedation, and now, they have him strapped and tied to a bed. I guess," Morrison paused to find the right phrase, "he went a little berserk."

"I guess so," Stratford agreed. "How about his wife, Joyce?"

"She's actually been no problem...unlike her husband. She hasn't done anything crazy, anyway. They also have her under sedation, and someone's been watching her. I think she just wants to get the hell out of here, and if you ask me, the sooner we get both of them off this ship, the better."

"I understand they're preparing the Romulus to remove them," Stratford informed Morrison, who nodded in agreement. "I'm not sure of the logistics involved, but I agree. I want them out of here as bad as you."

While both men talked, they had been gazing out the heavy window, observing the processing of the Olympia for long term storage. Several tow vehicles were being employed to pull the shuttle into the hangar where it would be kept. Stratford looked over to see one of the technicians electronically lower the thick metal door and the shuttle disappeared from view. It occurred to him that many years, many centuries, would pass before anyone might again sit at its controls, and the thought of it somehow startled him. Even so, at some incalculable moment in the future, he would instruct his son or daughter, or someone else's child, in the piloting of the shuttle to pass along the knowledge to another generation, and again the skills would be passed to yet another and another.

"Would you like to see him...talk to him, Captain?" Morrison asked.

"I suppose I should, yes," replied Stratford.

"Fine. Dr. Phen asked that I bring you first to him. I guess to brief you on the specifics regarding Bentz's condition."

It suddenly occurred to Stratford to remove his flight suit, discovering as he did the rumpled message from the President. He unfolded the paper and read it silently.

"What's that, David?" Morrison asked.

Stratford didn't answer immediately as he took in the words. "It's a message from the President. Hardin wrote this down last night and then gave it to me before takeoff because of the gag order," he said tersely, and handed it off to Morrison.

The actor read it and was visibly moved. "Damn," he shook his head. "That's powerful...I guess I never gave him much credit."

"Yeah...well, see to it that it's kept safe," Stratford said.

"Don't worry; I won't let anything happen to it. In fact, I'll put it in the archival display cabinet by the main corridor," Morrison promised, then folded it and put it in his own suit.

# Chapter 12

The two men left forthwith from the landing area and passed quickly to the main corridor that would lead them to the midsection of the Mayflower where the medical complex and related facilities were housed. It was obvious when they arrived that Dr. Phen had been expecting them, as he was seated in the administrative area.

"Captain Stratford," Dr. Phen smiled solicitously and rose to greet the Mayflower's commander. "Thank you too, Mr. Morrison, for bringing him. It is a pleasure, Captain, to see you again. I hope your flight was without incident?"

"Not so bad, really," he confirmed with a weary smile. "The only thing to worry about is the landing, but I understand the flight here was rough too."

"Oh yes…you are referring to our recent difficulties with poor Mr. Bentz…a terrible thing. Luckily, no one was hurt because of his tirade."

"Captain, Dr. Phen…excuse me," Morrison broke in. "I do want to look in on the recent arrivals and make sure they're getting settled."

"That's okay, John," Stratford dismissed Morrison with a casual wave. "I'll talk with you later."

After Morrison departed, the two men took seats opposite each other, and the doctor opened the discussion about the recent crisis.

"I understand, sir, based on recent communications from the WSO, the Romulus has departed. You might also be interested to know that the Bentz's will be escorted under benefit of armed guards. That is to say, Richard Bentz."

"Do you believe that's necessary?" Stratford asked, incredulous.

Dr. Phen shrugged. "Perhaps, perhaps not, it's not for me to say. Psychologically, I would rather Mr. Bentz not be subjected to it. It may further his distaste for the WSO and the Project, but until official inquiry is made, I think Hendrickson would prefer to take no chances."

"What do you mean by an 'official inquiry'?" Stratford asked.

"Thorough psychological evaluations for one thing and consultations with legal counsel, for another. I understand that Hendrickson wants this treated as a deliberate act of sabotage. At least, that's what he wants Bentz charged with."

"Sabotage…yeah…I guess so," Stratford said slowly, and shifted his weight in his chair, staring at, or perhaps through, Dr. Phen as he held his own private counsel. It could also be called attempted murder, multiple counts, he concluded. This sort of problem was the last thing they needed, and they hadn't yet broken free of their Earth-bound orbit. For the purpose of morale among the other crew members or because of the bad press this could generate on Earth, giving the doomsayers reason anew to openly criticize the WSO was simply something they did not need.

"I better at least see him, maybe speak to him. That is, unless you have any objections," Stratford said finally, acknowledging Phen's authority as Bentz's physician.

"No, I have no problem with that. In fact, Dr. Hardin was insistent you should. I have to warn you, though, at times he is wildly incoherent. He is on sedatives, which might have calmed him by now."

"What's your opinion, medical opinion, of him, doctor? Is he mentally ill?"

"Mentally ill?" Dr. Phen mused, as if trying to convince himself. "Psychologically, based on his behavior and certain things he has told me leads me to believe he is suffering from delusions of grandeur. He also believes he is omniscient, which means all knowing, god-like. In a word, Captain, he is a paranoid schizophrenic."

Stratford shook his head sympathetically. "The poor S.O.B., what's the outcome…ah…prognosis for something like that?"

"These things are hard to predict. In general, psychoses are difficult to treat. Drugs can make a tremendous difference in some individuals, while in others, very little. With best treatment, we might expect him to recover over time, but he could also grow much worse, as psychotic states are often progressive." Dr. Phen shrugged at the tangled paradoxes he was trying to describe. "However, Captain…if you will come with me, I will take you to his quarters."

# Chapter 13

Proceeding through the maze of corridors that connected the hospital complex, they entered a short passageway where the horticulturalist was being kept. Noticing a solitary nurse seated at a makeshift observation post outside his chamber, Stratford knew at once that they had arrived at Benz's location.

"Please excuse us, Sherry," the doctor addressed the nurse. "Oh, do you know each other?" he asked as a polite afterthought, and indeed, Lydia Stratford had shared a training session with Sherry Friesen, and the Captain did know her. "Captain Stratford has come to visit our patient. Have there been any changes in his condition?"

"No, doctor. He's been very subdued since his last injection of Thorazine."

Dr. Phen reached for the computerized patient log, and read silently over the entries the nurse had made since he last looked in on Bentz. Everything looked in order. Routinely, he continued his questions. "Has he eaten, requested anything, or made any comments?" Turning to Stratford, he explained his last question. "Hendrickson requested we record any comments Bentz might make."

Sherry responded in turn. "I looked in on him a while ago. I offered to have something to eat brought from the dining hall, but he wouldn't answer me."

"Was he asleep, perhaps," Dr. Phen asked.

"No, that's the weird part. It's in my logged notes, if you want to read them over. However, he was quite awake, I assure you. He watched me enter the room, and even turned his head to follow my movements, but he never said a word."

"Very strange, indeed," the doctor agreed.

"Very creepy, Doctor, if you ask me."

"I agree. You are welcome to take your leave now, Sherry. I will remain here until your replacement reports. Thank you so much."

"Fine. I'll do that. Captain, I'm glad you're finally aboard," Sherry said and then made her hasty departure.

Dr. Phen turned toward Stratford. "I guess you should go in. I will be outside here in case you need anything. Don't worry, though, he is tied quite securely to his bed. Actually, I will be recording the conversation if that's alright. Both Hardin and Hendrickson agreed it might be useful later."

Stratford knew that 'useful' meant 'legally useful' and reminded himself to choose his words carefully.

"I understand," he said and positioned his hand over the entry pad. The door slid silently open, admitting him to the room beyond. The small chamber was in semi-darkness, and he paused for his eyes to adjust. He noticed a figure lying flat in a bed in the far corner, shrouded in white sheets with heavy black strapping crisscrossing his chest, securing him to the bed.

"Richard?" Stratford said softly.

Bentz was studying his visitor carefully; he knew it was Captain Stratford. He expected him sooner.

"I understand you've had some problems," Stratford continued and felt ridiculous having said it. On the other hand, any comment under these circumstances would register as being inane.

"Yeah? Thank you for coming," the gardener said unexpectedly and vigorously, so much his response surprised Stratford. "Is that what you understand? Or, is that what you've been told? The real question is: is it really my problem or your problem," he sneered. "More to the point, maybe it's the WSO's problem, and they want to try and make it mine."

"Having tried to sabotage this ship. I'd say it's your problem," Stratford said with conviction. He was perfectly willing to parry.

"That's a very good answer, Colonel, and perhaps you're right. But please, you're making me uncomfortable standing there like that. By all means, please be seated. I don't mean to be a bad host. I'd have gotten up to greet you, but in case you haven't noticed, I'm rather preoccupied at the moment." At this, Bentz broke into a laugh, borne less of joy than a broken spirit. Stratford responded wordlessly by pulling a chair close to the bed.

"Would you like to tell me, Richard, why you did it? What was it you hoped to gain?"

Bentz remained silent for the space of nearly half a minute. "I was trying to rectify a mistake," he offered quietly.

"I was told you experienced a 'moral panic.' Would you explain that?"

"Colonel...it's the Mayflower Project itself, and I was trying to rectify a mistake."

"Whose mistake, Richard?" Stratford prodded. "Yours? The WSO's?"

Dr. Phen opened the door at that moment, and both Stratford and Bentz looked toward the source of the light. "Gentlemen, the escorts from the Romulus are here," Phen said to both, then addressed Bentz. "Richard, these men will be with you on your flight back to Earth."

Stratford noticed both of the burly guards had holstered pistols, and one carried a pair of handcuffs. "You were starting to tell me about the mistake, Richard. I just hope you realize what you did and the consequences. The Project is the greatest scientific—"

"Travesty," Bentz interrupted. "It's the greatest of all scientific travesties. That's what it is. But let me say good-bye here, Colonel David Stratford, and I hope...I hope you have a nice day."

Stratford left, retracing his path through the hospital complex. "Have a nice day...have a nice day...," he kept repeating to himself. "Have a...day...," then he remembered and felt through his WSO suit. "Damn it."

He still had his wrist watch.

# Chapter 14

"David, could you come in here?" Lydia Stratford called out weakly from the shower stall. Her voice was nearly inaudible, and her husband didn't hear her over the sound of the spraying water. She placed the palms of her hands against the shower wall behind her, steadying herself, as a second, sickening wave of nausea ran through her. Leaning back with knees buckled, she let the shower spray strike her upturned face, partially restoring her, yet she still felt fatigued. She eventually squeezed out. She shook her head gently from side to side, wet tangles of her hair snapped smartly on opposite shoulders. It occurred to her, *he didn't hear me,* she thought. She had recovered sufficiently to turn on the warm air jets, dried off, and stepped from the enclosure and into her robe. Weak as she was, she made it to the edge of the bed and sat down heavily, relieved. "What is this?" she asked herself aloud and apprehension replaced nausea as she inventoried the possibilities. "David," she called, and being closer to the living area of their quarters where he was, this time she made herself heard. "Could you come in here, please?"

As was his habit, Stratford had risen much earlier and was reviewing the latest response to his reports to the WSO on the computer. Behind him, the large TV screen wall monitor displayed an episode of *The Honeymooners*, the television show from the 1950s starring Jackie Gleason. He rarely activated the system to actually watch anything; rather, he kept the sound off allowing the sense of motion and light it gave the living area to strangely relax him. He looked up absently from his work and turned when Lydia called his name. "What is it?" he answered.

"Can you come in here?" Lydia stressed the word 'in,' her impatience obvious.

Stratford flipped the TV monitor off and rose to obey leaving the computer running. "What is it?" he asked again. Lydia looked up when he entered the bed chamber, and at a glance, he needed no explanation to know something wasn't right.

"I don't know, really. It's just that I feel awful. Could you call the hospital and tell them I won't be able to go on duty?"

Stratford stood close and stroked Lydia's damp hair away from her forehead. No temperature, he was relieved to find out. "If you're not feeling well, don't you think you should go over there anyway and let them take a look at you?"

"I'm sure I'll feel better if I can just stay in bed awhile," Lydia rationalized.

"Well…what exactly…how do you feel?"

"I really don't know what this is. I felt a little like this before I went on duty last. Do you suppose it could be some sort of flu?"

"According to what the WSO told us, it can't be. At the very least, it's not supposed to be, considering all those damned inoculations we had. They also sterilized the ship piece by piece before it was sent out into space and assembled, so it can't be that." Neither of them said anything for a moment, both being unwilling to discuss the uglier, more ominous possibilities.

Stratford sat down beside Lydia. "I think you should get dressed, and I'll walk you over there. Unless, you prefer breakfast first."

"Oh, David, are you kidding?" she groaned, laying her head against his arm. "I'm not up for any food…not right now, anyway. Maybe, I'll feel better if I just stay in bed and rest. I really hate to make a big deal out of a little…"

Reacting to her reluctance to seek help, Stratford slipped into character, for levity's sake. "One of these days, Alice," he growled in his best Ralph Kramden imitation and swung his left fist in an exaggerated uppercut. "Bang – zoom! To the moon!"

Lydia giggled appreciatively at his display. "Yeah, sure, you big lug." She was willing to play Alice to David's Ralph. "Do you have any idea how far past the moon we are now, slugger?"

Well, actually he did. As Captain of the Mayflower, he had a damned good idea. Indeed, they were over sixteen months into the Project, and in fact, a billionish miles beyond the moon. Even still, the ship had not yet reached the maximum velocity projected by the WSO engineers of 240,000 miles per hour, which would require a few more months to accomplish.

Adapting to life aboard a space craft, they had quickly discarded the earthly concept of days and nights as measured in twenty-four-hour increments.

Instead, they found it convenient to order events based on work schedules but retained seconds, minutes, and hours as a useful "fractional currency." In outer space, though, a day/night made no sense. When needed, they could refer to the atomic clocks, which marked the passage of time for posterity as well as for the official tally. As the Mayflower crept forward, time inevitably flowed in space as on Earth.

"Fair enough, Alice," Stratford laughed and left Lydia alone to dress. "I'm walking you to the hospital," he reiterated firmly. When his voice took on a particular tone, she knew there would be no further debate. "It's better to get this checked; you're a nurse. I don't have to tell you that. If it turns out to be some sort of infection, you should be on an antibiotic as soon as possible."

"I know, I know," Lydia agreed reluctantly.

Stratford proceeded to call the hospital, apprising them of the recent development with Lydia.

"Clinic," a woman's voice stated. It was Pamela Reddie.

"This is Captain Stratford, Pam. I'm—"

"Oh, hello, Captain, what can I do for you?"

"Nothing…nothing for me. I'm calling for Lyddie. She's not feeling well. She probably won't be able to work her shift either, but I wanted her to come in and get checked out. Is that okay?"

"Certainly, that's fine; just bring her over. What seems to be wrong with her?"

"Ah, well…I'm not entirely sure," Stratford confessed. "She was feeling lousy, nauseous, and I just want to make sure she has it checked out. So please, don't let her talk you into giving her an aspirin or something."

"Don't worry, Captain," Pam said, slightly amused. "We'll be very thorough, I promise you. Generally, we run enough tests to rule out most—"

"Who's the doctor on duty?" Stratford asked suddenly.

"It's Dr. Hester. Why?"

*Great*, he thought. Dr. Jason Hester, that son of a bitch. He dismissed Pam's question out of hand, however, not wanting to let his personal feelings known. "What? Oh, no reason really. I was just wondering."

"Who are you talking to, David?" Lydia said as she entered the living area, combing her still damp hair.

"Hold a second, Pam." Stratford placed a hand over the receiver. "It's Pam Reddie. Are you ready to go?"

"Actually, I'm feeling pretty good now, so maybe I'll be able to go on duty after all."

"Yeah, that's wonderful," Stratford declared in mock agreement. "Listen up, Alice. You're going to the hospital but strictly as an inmate." He gave his wife a withering look, non-verbally restating his disapproval, then turned his attention back to the phone. "Pam, I'm still here. Sorry. Yes, yes, of course. We'll be there shortly."

# Chapter 15

The couple left their quarters and entered the main concourse that led to the hospital. It was located where the four avenues of the ship intersected, and their approach was from the starboard arc, passing the cafeteria on the way.

Stratford took Lydia's arm as they walked. He knew she wasn't prone to overstate a minor ailment, prompting his solicitous concern for her. Despite the Mayflower's well-equipped hospital and pharmacy, he realized some medical conditions could arise that although easily treatable on Earth could be life threatening in deep space. Looking affectionately at her, he squeezed her arm a little tighter.

The entrance way to the cafeteria was bustling with at least two dozen crew members arriving for their meals. Some were at the conclusion of their shifts while others were awaiting their next assignment. Among them were John and Christine Morrison. Since the Mayflower's departure, it had become an established ritual between the Stratford's and the Morrison's to share a breakfast table, and consequently, a warm friendship developed. While David Stratford at first glance appeared easy to know, having a relaxed style and easy manner, he was paradoxically difficult to actually know well. He tended to withdraw from deep intimacies. He genuinely liked John Morrison's unassuming personality, which was unusual for an actor. His solid foundation extended to the spouses as well.

"Good morning, you two," John Morrison smiled as the Stratford's came closer. "We were beginning to wonder if we'd be alone for breakfast. Glad to see you could make it."

Lydia and Christine had clasped hands in greeting. "Actually," Lydia began ruefully, "we were on our way to the hospital not to report for duty. I wasn't feeling very well this morning, and David insisted I should at least go in and get checked."

"Lydia!" Christine exclaimed. "What on Earth is wrong?"

Stratford spoke up, cutting off his wife's response. She recognized that his serious tone was put-on. "Ahh...well, you might stand corrected there, Christine."

"Really? How so?"

"What on Mayflower is wrong, I believe you meant to say."

"Very clever. You're very funny, Captain," Christine smiled agreeably. Lydia shook her head, and John grimaced. "However, I must disagree with you," Christine continued. "The real answer is: everything. Everything on Earth is wrong. Don't you agree? Or else we wouldn't be here, right?"

Stratford had no answer for that. In basic principle, though, he didn't disagree with her. If the members of the Mayflower Project had been polled, they wouldn't have disagreed, either. In the United States at least, a mindless permissiveness had gradually replaced common sense, making all manner of reprehensible behaviors acceptable, if not fashionable. Criminal sociopathy was the new celebrity. Ravenous consumerism, no longer merely conspicuous, substituted happiness, and the pursuit of greed justified any means achieving it. Mediocrity had become the new standard of excellence, as America willingly imploded upon itself. For these Mayflower expatriates, however, the tenuousness of life in deep space ever reminded them of their human frailties – and that ultimately it was only life itself that mattered.

Proceeding toward the hospital complex, the Stratford's were loudly greeted by the physician on duty, Dr. Jason Hester, who was seated at the reception desk. Lydia entered first, and Hester looked up from his reading materials. "Lydia, my dear, you are looking lovely," he proclaimed, and he was more than a little surprised to see Stratford was present too. "And, yes, of course, forgive me. Greetings to the Supreme Commander of the Mayflower," he added sardonically.

Stratford held a low opinion of Hester. He was, for one thing, monumentally arrogant, believing himself to possess a rare medical genius, but he also imagined himself as an irresistible Lothario. During the early planning stages of the Mayflower Project, he had briefly been considered as a candidate for command of the Mayflower, but Hardin rejected him, having rightly sensed that he was little more than a well-crafted façade. Since then, he maintained a subtly contemptuous attitude toward the Captain, which was demonstrated by the overblown salutation he gave him.

"Lydia, dear, I understand you're not feeling yourself," Hester continued. She noticeably recoiled from his unwelcome caress of her shoulders. "Please," and he nodded toward Pamela Reddie, who had entered from the nurse's station. "Pam has already set up for your exam. Go ahead with her. Captain, you're certainly welcome to join us," the Doctor said and dropped his arm from Lydia's shoulders, encircling her waist for a brief moment before she broke free and fell in step behind Pam.

"No, I don't think so," Stratford's voice sounded constricted. "Lydia," he called to his wife, "I'll catch up with you later. I want to talk to the doctor for a moment." He stepped toward the outside corner of the corridor leading to the examination rooms. Hester's inquiring look gave way to one of shocked surprise as Stratford's stiffened arm shot out and pinned Hester's shoulder against the bulkhead behind him. The muffled thump his body made as it contacted the steel wall caused Lydia to glance back, but her husband and the doctor were effectively hidden from sight.

"Do your job," Stratford said quietly.

"Captain?" Hester said inquiringly, taken aback. Yet, he knew what this was about.

"Do your job," the Captain repeated. "Just do your job. Do what you were assigned to do," and he relaxed the pressure on Hester's shoulder but still kept him immobile. "Nothing else. You signed on as a physician, so be one."

Droplets of nervous perspiration had formed on Hester's forehead. "Of course, Captain, of course," he whined. "I am…I mean, I will check Lydia over thoroughly. Please not to worry about that."

That wasn't it. Stratford tilted his head slightly to look straight into Hester's eyes. Deceit? He decided to let it go. There was no point in debating. They both knew exactly what this was about.

"Good," Stratford forced a smile and took his hand from the doctor's shoulder.

The Alpha order was reaffirmed.

"I have some other things to do, but I'll try to get back here and if not…"

"If not, I understand, Captain," Hester completed the sentence, but not the thought. Stratford let this go, too. "We will probably perform several basic tests and others as needed. We can alert you over the PA system when, how, and where, if you'd like."

Stratford nodded.

"Rest assured; Lydia will receive the best possible care available in the known universe."

# Chapter 16

Stratford returned to the cafeteria after leaving the hospital. He passed through the service entrance directly into the kitchen. Frannie Collins, the jovial food operations manager, was visibly startled by his unexpected appearance as she turned from the steaming pots on the massive stove before her.

"Oh my...it's you, Captain," Frannie exclaimed loudly and clutched at her upper chest. "You scared the shit out of me, I swear."

"Sorry, I didn't mean to. I thought I'd come in to..."

"You're not supposed to be on duty here, are you?" Frannie questioned.

"No. You're right. Today I'm supposed to be the Commander of the Known Universe. Tomorrow I'm the bus boy," Stratford joked playfully. "I just came in to fix myself some breakfast."

The designers of the Mayflower Project had realized that in order to maintain a minimal crew, it would be necessary for labor and maintenance tasks to be shared. This would give them some respite from their duties. Stratford rather enjoyed his kitchen assignments.

Frannie watched in silent amusement as Stratford rummaged for a bowl. Then, he dipped into the large holding bin for a portion of dried oatmeal. "Captain, I'd be happy to do that for you," she offered.

"Thanks, but I'm almost ready here," he replied distantly as he estimated a cup of water and stirred it into the oats. Satisfied, he popped open the door of the nearest microwave oven.

Unable to contain herself, Frannie wiped her hands and shook her head doubtfully, she nudged Stratford aside. "It's a good thing you only come in here to clean up because you don't have any idea what you're doing. You need more water in there," she admonished, dispensing the needed amount. "Get out of here, please, Captain. Go sit in the dining hall, and I'll bring it to you."

Stratford did as he was told.

John Morrison was seated alone in the dining area and waved the Captain over to join him. "So, what's the word on Lydia?" Morrison asked. "Did they find out anything yet?"

Meanwhile, Frannie approached the table with Stratford's breakfast.

"Here you are, hot and healthy," she said cheerily, but then her tone turned serious. "I wanted to ask you how Lydia is doing, Captain. Any word?"

Both Stratford and Morrison looked at the woman with astonishment.

"To be honest, I really don't know yet," Stratford offered slowly. "But how is it? I don't understand. You actually heard us talking from…how did you know anything was wrong with her?"

Frannie laughed aloud. "Well, this isn't that big of a ship, for one thing, and when the Captains' First Lady takes ill, believe me, it's newsworthy. News travels fast, faster than this ship, maybe."

"In that case, to answer your question, I don't know anything except they were going to run some tests, and go from there."

"What was her problem?" Frannie asked.

"She said she woke up this morning not feeling well, nauseous."

Frannie gazed for a moment off into the distance, trying to form an answer, an opinion, or both. Instead, she settled for another question. "Was this the first time she felt like this?"

"No, actually it wasn't. She felt a little poorly yesterday morning, too."

"Is that so? Well, I wouldn't worry too much, Captain," Frannie said mysteriously. "I'm sure she's fine."

"Thanks for your optimism. I hope you're right because I can't help thinking about the worst case."

"But that's just it, Captain," Frannie interrupted. "There's two things you need: one of them is optimism, for sure, and the other is to eat your breakfast before it gets cold," she added severely.

Stratford could hardly think of an appropriate response except to hold up a spoonful of steaming oatmeal in agreement with her. He then flashed an obedient smile. Satisfied her words had the desired effect, Frannie departed to complete her work in the kitchen.

John Morrison immediately changed the subject. "I probably better leave, too. You want to come with me? I'm having rehearsals for the play I'm putting on. Hell, maybe you'll even want to be in it."

"I wish I could, but I'm making some rounds today," Stratford said regretfully. "So, what's the play?"

"Oh, it's this comedy I wrote called 'The Monkey Cage.' It has a really cute premise. This scientist teaches a monkey to speak, and pretty soon the monkey becomes smarter than the scientist, so they agree to switch places. So, now the monkey is running things, including..."

"Hey, it sounds interesting, but don't ruin it for me," Stratford protested. "There won't be any point in seeing it if I already know all the details."

John and Christine Morrison's role as the Mayflower's historians was undemanding compared to being the entertainment officers. They weighed the relative impact of events and recorded them as they happened into the ship's permanent log. So far, the most noteworthy entry was the birth of the first Mayflower baby, Virginia Dare Perry, daughter of Charles and Lisa Perry, both from maintenance/food services. The child's name was an obvious tribute to the first child of European descent born in North America at Roanoke in 1587. Being cause for wild celebration aboard ship, the story had a strangely mixed and surreal effect on certain Earthlings. Some visionaries embraced the birth as a grand furtherance of mankind by exporting the species to new worlds, and there were those who argued that a primary quality of "humanness" required being born on Earth. For them, the child's extraterrestrial pedigree constituted the origin of a new species, *Homo aloftus*, and was one more reason to denigrate the Project and the WSO.

For the expatriates, the only news from Earth that held their interest was the fate of Richard Bentz. Dr. Hardin's official report on behalf of the WSO to Captain Stratford stated that Bentz had been adjudged insane. Indeed, the grainy film of Bentz's disembarkment from the Romulus showed a handcuffed, disheveled, and wild-eyed repatriate, which visually supported the contention of insanity. Consequently, Hardin had him placed in the deepest, darkest recesses of an impenetrable mental hospital, precluding any legal charges that might have been brought against him.

This was the fanciful, WSO version of what happened, approved by Robert Hendrickson and sanitized for the minds of the Mayfloridians. Apparently, Einstein was only partially correct with his General Theory of Relativity; time and truth can both vary, relative to the frame of reference.

The actual truth read...differently.

Bentz's team of lawyers plotted his defense upon his arrival by initiating a trial by tabloids. They rationalized his actions based on, or courtesy thereof, a quasi-religious higher calling, inadvertently creating a movement of rapturous followers. Once the trial began, he was represented as more mischievous than Machiavellian, less Cosa Nostra than Our Gang. He was, however, found guilty of attempted sabotage and endangering the lives of the Mayflower men and women. The sentence he drew was only a lengthy probation term. Society valued his celebrity status more than it needed to punish him for his notoriety. As for his wife, Joyce was cleared of any involvement or culpability at the very outset.

After Richard's trial, the couple undertook a personal crusade maligning the WSO, and Hardin and Hendrickson were powerless to stop it. However, they could not alter or affect the Project. The Mayflower, like a beam of light, was self-propagating and not subject to recall. Their efforts did, however, help quash another long-range colonization the WSO had tentatively planned to the star system B.D. +43B in the Constellation Lacerta. This ended up making Bentz partly successful after all. Thereafter, the WSO, personified by Bob Hendrickson, chairman, was resigned to chartering exotic vacations for mega-wealthy dilettantes to and from the permanent enclave the WSO had constructed on Mars. It was sad, in a way. The age of scientifically-driven space explorations had ended with the Mayflower Project, and now, they were forced to become profitable.

# Chapter 17

The Captain and John Morrison parted company. Morrison's destination was the auditorium, while Stratford proceeded aft, following the main concourse. He intended to look in on Michael Woofter and his domain. Everyone had come to refer to it as simply "the garden," which of course, it was. Although in scope and purpose, it seemed deserving of a more grandiose title since it provided all, or almost all, of their vital requirements.

Stratford entered the garden. Then, he quickly took in the office of operations, finding it empty. He guessed that Woofter was likely inside the garden complex and went to the large observation window that gave view to the living domain within. As always, taken by the commanding visual presence that was just beyond that glass, he hardly knew where to look. The Mayflower's garden was the only natural wonder, unnatural as it seemed aboard this ship, for these travelers to gaze upon. As expected, everyone had quickly tired of the black, unchanging vastness of the universe visible through the portals. Stratford and his entire crew were often drawn to the garden and marveled at this lush, life-sustaining world in microcosm. Its subtle array of greens – emerald, aqua, seafoam, blue – reminded them or at least Stratford that the only thing about planet Earth worth missing was planet Earth itself.

The horticulturalist was nowhere in sight. Given the size of the complex, Woofter could have been anywhere within it. Stratford reached below the window, feeling for a large red button set in a control panel and pressed it twice, thereby activating the garden's signal horn. There was a barely audible throaty roar that reverberated through the garden. Its echoes repeated, then grew softer until they expired. This system had been designed to alert anyone in the garden complex from the office, minimizing the opening of the double set of air-lock doors. This prevented the spread of pollen or the escape of errant members of the bee colony from infiltrating the rest of the ship.

Woofter materialized out of the foggy mist and approached the office, head down, dressed in raingear that glistened wet. He glanced up briefly to see who had summoned him and recognizing the Captain standing at the observation glass, gave a cheery wave. He entered the air-lock and began peeling off his outer clothing, shaking off the water, and hanging them on hooks to dry.

"Hello, Captain," he said loudly, his voice pitched in a higher register to carry through the bulkhead. "Hold on, I'll be with you shortly." He activated the air-lock's inner door, then stepped out and stood before Stratford. As usual, the gardener was smiling broadly, which Stratford found disconcerting. Every other passenger, including the Captain, had adapted sufficiently to life aboard the Mayflower, finding contentment in their purpose. However, Woofter seemed genuinely happy. "Everything is okay, I hope, Captain?" Woofter inquired. The two men clasped hands.

"Yeah, there's no problem, Michael. I just hope I didn't call you away from anything important."

Michael reassured him he had not.

"This is just routine," Stratford continued, "but maybe you can answer the same question. How's everything going out here?"

"Fine and good. The garden grows fine, and I generally have more helpers than I need. Everyone likes this assignment so much. I suppose it's because it reminds them of home. If you'll be patient with me, Captain, I need to log in." Stratford's look amounted to permission and so Woofter took his seat at the computer console. "I just need to log in a few numbers," he said by way of clarification.

The Captain absently walked around the office. The room was designed as the center of operations for the entire garden. A great many conduits with countless valves to modify or control the flow were affixed to bulkhead and ceiling alike. At the rear wall, he noticed a heavy door constructed of thick steel, being substantial in height as well as width. It had a large square key pad above its handle, and lights indicated that the mechanism, a time lock, was activated.

"What's in this chamber?" he asked the gardener. "Do you know?"

"Pardon me, Captain?" Woofter tossed off casually over his shoulder without breaking his gaze with the computer monitor.

"I said, what do you suppose is in this chamber, this room?"

Woofter turned to look. "Well, that's a very good question, sir. I only know it has a large supply of seeds held in specially designed freezers for long-term storage. However, I can't say for sure what else might be in there."

Stratford pointed at the time lock, then rapped lightly with his knuckle on the heavy door. "This is a little drastic, don't you think? Why did they feel the need to put them under such extreme security measures?"

Woofter smiled broadly before he spoke. "Who knows, Captain? Maybe they sent along some Cannabis seeds too," he said, as he consciously suppressed an urge to laugh at his witticism in front of the captain.

"Cannabis?" Stratford repeated. "You mean marijua…"

"Yes, marijuana, but I'm just kidding, sir," Woofter explained. "Actually, I suppose they're seeds the WSO knew would be unmanageable aboard ship, such as trees. They would have sent them for the last generation, I guess, who'll plant them once they reach Earth 2."

Stratford nodded, conceding the logic in that.

"By the way, Captain, you might find this interesting. Did you know the time lock is deactivated by the pull of gravity? I think that is amazing. Brilliant. Once the Mayflower approaches its destination, the lock will automatically disengage."

"That is amazing," Stratford agreed but actually failed to answer the gardener's question. As Captain, he knew. There was a chamber like this one just off the main control room, the ship's bridge, and it was also secured by a lock like this one. The difference was the WSO had entrusted Stratford with detailed knowledge of the room's contents as well as the means to override the time lock should the need to do so occur. Not that it was any of Woofter's business.

Suddenly a voice, filtered and compressed, yet recognizable as that of Steve Lester, first officer, came out of the public address system.

"Captain Stratford…urgent. Please proceed at once to the bridge. Repeat. Urgent. Captain Stratford, please report to the bridge."

The gardener looked inquiringly at Stratford; eyebrows raised. Stratford responded with a shrug, but the gesture was more to himself. He left the office in stride, hardly glancing at Woofter. Within a few footsteps, Hester's excited voice repeated the message. Having now provoked curiosity among the ship's company, and for some, fear, many stepped into the main concourse to watch Stratford pass. Maintenance and kitchen workers stood silently as he approached, not unlike as on Earth when a police siren induces a morbid fascination.

# Chapter 18

Lester had observed proper protocol. *His voice conveyed excitement and not panic*, Stratford thought. He had also avoided using the word "emergency," and so the Captain concluded this was more likely about a matter of policy he was being summoned. He hoped. Passing these onlookers, he felt a heightened responsibility toward all of them, as their Captain. His greatest duty was to the Mayflower Project; somehow, it seemed it had gradually become that, over the last billion or so miles. Even as he approached the hospital, he suppressed an urge to inquire about Lydia. He bowed his head as he passed some new members to avoid their frightened gazes and quickened his pace to a jog.

Upon entering the control room, he witnessed a scene of uncharacteristic activity. Usually, there might be only one person on duty. The Mayflower's computer-driven auto pilot system knew where it was going and required only occasional adjustments to the flight plan. This time, Ramon da Silva was seated at the control panel of the Deep Observation Guidance monitor, DOG, for short. Next to him was Steve Lester. The room had also gathered some curious bystanders as all news on a space craft was noteworthy, whether good or bad.

"Captain," Steve Lester stood quickly and gestured over the heads of the spectators once Stratford entered. He had kept vigil for his arrival with one eye, while simultaneously watching the DOG. The function of the Deep Observational Guidance system was to scan the space in the Mayflower's path using a radar-based imagery process to prevent collisions with all manner of space debris. Should even the smallest object strike the ship at the speed they traveled, the impact would be comparable to a sizeable boulder striking a sheet of paper. Once the presence of an object was confirmed, a series of powerful lasers could be employed to blast the offending object into dust. For larger threats, such as an asteroid, the lasers could affect a new trajectory, pushing it into a new path, allowing the ship to pass harmlessly by.

"You've got to see this," Lester exulted.

The crowd parted respectfully as Stratford came closer. "What's this about?" he asked tersely.

"Watch the DOG monitor," da Silva said. Realizing that hardly qualified as an answer, Ramon elaborated further. "I suppose the system registered a presence out there because of its size. When I first resolved the image, it appeared to be a space craft, but I lost it." He paused, making further adjustments to the controls by pressing some buttons in rapid succession, while others he tapped once or twice. His efforts to conjure up the mysterious image again was rewarded when the screen flickered for a moment. Then it went black. "It appears to be about…I'd say…550,000 miles away," he continued. "It's at an oblique angle to our flight path, the best I can tell, so I doubt there's any danger of a collision." There had reappeared an insignificant smudge of light with a dark background in the center of the monitor, and Stratford leaned over.

"That doesn't look like a space ship to me, or anything for that matter," he observed wryly.

"Watch the screen," da Silva instructed.

"You said you were able to resolve an image before?"

"Yes, sir," da Silva acknowledged firmly.

"Would you say, then, it was alien?"

"Alien?" the technician repeated with a hint of sarcasm. "Hell, out here, you could say we're 'alien' ourselves, sir, but I know what you meant." He pondered the question again before answering. "I really couldn't say for sure either way, Captain."

He turned back to his task, and in the breathless silence that followed, the gathering watched him tweak the system, cajole it, attempting to lock in a viable image. Suddenly, the screen filled with an ivory-colored presence of sorts. No one knew quite what to make of it, resembling, for lack of a better comparison, the saucer to a tea cup.

Strange.

"What the hell is that?" Lester demanded rhetorically.

"Back it off. Back it off," da Silva admonished himself. The coordinates now read the same as when he first detected the object, and he knew he was on the right track. The equipment responded to his deft touch, shrinking the image instantly down to a hundredth of its former size, becoming absorbed into a larger, horrific sight. Everyone gasped in recognition: this was a human face.

Seemingly molded from a creamy white wax and rendered in perfect detail, it was grotesque, surreal, and out of context in deep space. The mouth was hung partly open, passive and silent, while the face itself wore no expression. Framed by a space helmet, ice crystals formed a coating along the edge of the glass shield.

They continued to stare in perverse amazement. Ramon had begun twisting an array of knobs, which caused the first image of the saucer to alternate back and forth with the face as he tried to reconcile these seemingly unrelated pictures into a paradigm of logic.

Steve Lester grasped the relationship between them. "That saucer-shaped thing; you know what that is? It's a close-up of the face's left eye," he observed excitedly, looking aside at Ramon for confirmation and over his shoulder at Captain Stratford for approval. A few people in the gathered crowd murmured their agreement.

Stratford had become detached from the others' conversations, following instead his own suspicions and intuition. "Ramon, let's take a wider look here and see what else we find in that cockpit."

Ramon obeyed, and he produced an altered view with the slightest adjustment. "There's...two. No, wait...there's another behind that second one, further back. It looks like four altogether," he summarized for the benefit of the assemblage, and he was correct. There were three more lifeless forms, all having died in an apparent instant, even as they performed their tasks.

"I'll say one thing for you, Ramon," Lester declared. "At least you weren't lying or hallucinating."

"That's actually two things," da Silva returned.

"I'm not sure I'm believing this," Stratford said slowly. "Can you scan the outside?"

The DOG system took into view the entire space craft as Ramon again complied.

"Look at those markings; that's WSO hardware," Lester exclaimed. "See? Look at the tail section, the trident insignia. I'll be damned. That's the..."

"It's the Neptune," Stratford completed Lester's sentence. "That first...astronaut, that's Hayden MacNeil."

"Yes, Captain," Chapman Collins agreed, pushing forward to take a closer look. "And that one there on the left is John Sanchez, the poor bastard."

"Looks like we found the Neptune," Lester said, sounding unconvinced of it himself. Realizing, perhaps, it was a bit like discovering a particular grain of sand that had been hidden on a beach…somewhere…along the Pacific Ocean. "But what happened to it?" he continued. "And why is it out here? It would have been adrift now for five or six years, and all that time everyone just assumed it had been destroyed."

"I can show you, Steve, what happened," da Silva offered. "I don't know if you saw this earlier, but let's take a look at her midsection." He began fine-tuning the system, bringing into view a sharp close-up of at least a dozen baseball-sized holes along the port side of the ship. "It looks to me like it caught some flak, for sure. Judging by the size, I'd say it was a hail of small asteroids that broadsided her."

"That's probably right, because it would have emptied the cabin of atmosphere in a matter of seconds; they'd have been frozen to death before they knew what hit them," Lester concluded and slumped back in his chair, looking blankly at the derelict space craft.

The Neptune had been the first of three space shuttles designed and built by the WSO that included the identical Olympia and Romulus. Commanded by Major Hayden MacNeil, the Neptune was lost on her maiden expedition. Its mission was to test the Deep Observational Guidance system and its associated lasers, which was the technology needed to ensure the Mayflower's safe passage. It was no small irony that the very system they were testing and which obviously failed them, was the same that led to their discovery.

"I'm going to put this over the closed-circuit TV," da Silva announced as he engaged the necessary components. "The rest of the crew will want to see what we found." He proceeded to describe the discovery over the sound system, but as the gathered spectators dispersed back to their posts, the news had already been disseminated thoroughly.

"Captain, the WSO will want to know about this, and they'll want pictures to verify…"

"Yes," Stratford cut Ramon short. "I'm sure they will, but send only those of the Neptune itself."

"Why not send them all?" the second officer demanded. "They're gonna want all that we have."

"I'm sure they would," Stratford agreed. "And if we sent them, you both know how things are on Earth. Those pictures of the crew will end up in some damned tabloid or for sale on eBay." His voice grew softer as he continued. "The people on that ship have families, kids. I know Hayden's wife, Carole, and his children, and I don't want them to see him like that. They died as heroes, as far as I'm concerned, and if we send pictures of them back to Earth, they won't be heroes. They'll just be corpses." He glanced down quickly at the monitor and looked at MacNeil. He suddenly felt like an intruder, a grave robber.

There was cause for Stratford's strong reaction to the discovery of the Neptune, as Ramon suddenly recalled. He had nearly taken command of the mission, but it was scheduled too closely to his return from Mars. There was also the impending Mayflower Project, so Stratford declined. It was upon his recommendation that Major MacNeil was chosen by the WSO. Ramon knew that both men had a shared NASA experience, but more than that, the two had been friends. As a result of these choices, Stratford's decision undeniably resulted in MacNeil's death.

Ramon understood the depth of despair that caused Stratford's comments, so he edited the visual display as requested. As he prepared the dispatch, Stratford made his departure.

# Chapter 19

The response that Stratford received at the hospital when he inquired about Lydia's condition was that she had been released by Dr. Hester with instructions to rest. When he entered their cabin, he assumed she would be asleep and was surprised to find her not only awake but sitting in the large chair, watching TV.

"Hey, I just came from the clinic. I thought for sure I'd find you sleeping," he said in an exaggerated reproachful tone.

"I was told to rest," she brightly corrected him. "But I'm really not tired. Just because you're supposed to rest doesn't necessarily mean 'sleep,' does it?"

"I guess not," Stratford conceded to his wife's logic without examining it too closely.

"Besides, who can sleep? I heard about the discovery of the Neptune, David, and I've been waiting for you to fill me in on the details."

Stratford sat down lightly on the edge of the armrest. "I suppose you've seen the footage Ramon pulled in?" he asked.

"Yes," Lydia answered, but then awaited an explanation.

"Well, that's pretty much it," he said briskly. "You know about as much as I do, then. They must have had a failure to their Guidance system because the side of the ship was riddled with holes."

"What caused the holes?" Lydia speculated. "Could it have been aliens?"

"Aliens?" Stratford laughed, and caressed the back of Lydia's neck. "Ahh…I doubt it. I think there's a better chance it was renegade Indians."

"Well, what then?" Lydia asked defensively.

"Small asteroids, by all indications."

"It's too bad," she said sadly. She knew the discovery of the Neptune could invoke old feelings of guilt and recriminations for her husband. She took his hands in hers." I'm sorry, David."

Stratford's response seemed callous as he pushed sentimentality aside. "They knew what could happen. Hayden was the kind of man who would...well, anyway. He knew the risks."

They all knew the risks.

"I'm sure the WSO will be pleased about our discovery," he continued. "Ramon is sending some of the pictures back to Earth. At least now, they'll know what happened. The families will be relieved too. Of course, we're not expecting a response from them anytime soon. It could take ten or more days to receive an acknowledgment."

"Ten days?" Lydia said in amazement. "I had no idea."

Stratford nodded. "Lester says every time we send a message it takes a little longer, and the signal is a little weaker. Maybe this time...who knows? Maybe we won't even..." His voice trailed off as he turned his attention to the TV. "I see they're showing *The Terminator* again."

The scene that was playing showed Los Angeles after the ascension of the computers over mankind, and machines had laid waste to the city leaving a landscape of burnt-out vehicles and human remains. *The Terminator* was one of the more popular films aboard, and John Morrison screened it regularly, mostly because it had not been edited as drastically as some other movies or TV shows. Dr. Hardin had ordered all objectionable scenes expunged from the Mayflower's library of DVDs, but the offensive material was not of violence or even sexually explicit footage. It was scenery of Earth; landscapes: forest, mountains, lakes, and even the sun and sky were removed. While *The Terminator* was edited, it retained the ghastly footage of Los Angeles under siege. Even films with fake scenery or painted backdrops were altered, while actors played out the action against a blackened background.

Hardin had theorized that alternatives fuel rebellion. Choices. For Aborigine tribesmen in the Amazon jungle or Eskimos living at the Artic Circle, to garner your child's devotion to the chosen life is to limit exposure to outside influences. He had become convinced that the future generations of Mayfloridians would also 'benefit' from sheltering them from knowledge of their Earthly heritage, and thereby engendering a deep, unwavering loyalty to the Project.

"So, what did Hester find out?" Stratford finally broached the topic of Lydia's health.

"Apart from insisting I get more rest, he said I have a…sort of infection," Lydia said mysteriously.

"An infection? How's that possible? The Mayflower was assembled under sterile conditions, and we all underwent preventative antibiotic therapy to rid us of bacteria and viruses, so that doesn't make a whole lot of sense," Stratford loudly protested.

"Actually, Dr. Hester said you gave it to me," and she threw a playfully disgusted look at her husband who paled slightly.

"I gave it to you? Are you telling me I have an infection too?" he demanded.

Well, it's more like an af-fection, I suppose, than an in-fection," she said, emphasizing the 'af' and 'in' prefixes.

"Okay. Can you explain what the hell that's supposed to mean? Is it something I should be treated for too? A virus? Or is it more like some sort of bacteria? Or what?"

Lydia could not maintain the charade any longer and began to giggle at her husband's predicament.

"No, David," she blurted out. "It's more like a…it's a baby. I'm pregnant."

# Chapter 20

Young David Stratford had pulled on his gold and black uniform, and looked pensively at his father, who was seated at the computer in their cabin. The child came closer, taking the smaller seat beside him. Having misunderstood the answer to a question he asked a moment earlier, he endeavored to present it again, slightly altered, if not more emphatic. "But what is the name of the place, daddy?"

"I already told you, Son, it's called Tau Ceti. That's the name of the star."

"And that's where we'll live?"

He stopped what he was doing and looked down and smiled at the inquisitive boy. "No, we won't live on it, first of all," the Father said patiently. "You can't live on a star, it's too hot. It's actually so hot you'd burn up if you got too close. There are two planets that orbit, which means 'to go around' Tau Ceti, and they're called Earth 2.0 and Earth 3.0" and he crudely illustrated the concept by holding up his son's closed fist as he passed his own index finger in a path around it. "You see? And people can live on the planets."

Caught up in the visual demonstration, the child failed to notice his father had effectively avoided answering his second question, too. "Which one will we live on?"

"Well, the only thing we know for sure is that both of them can support life, but the final decision will be made once the Mayflower gets closer so that tests can be made of each of their environments."

That sounded vague to the child. "Does that mean we'll all live on the same one?"

His father had to tread lightly now. "Of course, David, why wouldn't we?" the elder Stratford asked suspiciously, wondering where this line of questioning was coming from.

"Cause Stevie Lester says we'll never get there," the child blurted out excitedly. "He said none of us will, and I just wanted…"

"Where did he hear that?" Stratford demanded.

"His dad told him."

Damn it. That wasn't the right protocol, not for children this young. There was an outline set forth by the WSO to properly reveal the truths about the Project to the children. Stratford made a mental note to take this up later with Steve Lester. He then leaned over and gently lifted the boy from his chair and pulled him close. "Listen to me, David," he said softly. "We're aboard the Mayflower. This is our home, our world. We're safe, and we're healthy. We will always be together. Do you understand?"

The boy nodded that he did, but kept his eyes averted.

"We're part of an inherited commitment, which makes the Mayflower Project possible; everyone aboard has their special place in each other's lives. We all help make the Mayflower Project work, even though it is true we ourselves won't reach the final destination. But we will share in the glory of that moment through our children because the Mayflower Project will be mankind's greatest scientific achievement."

The child had listened carefully. "What's 'herited' mean?"

"It means – the word is 'inherited'; it means 'passed down from parent to child.'" He was unsure if the boy was old enough for all of this, but it was his best effort at damage control to undo Lester's irresponsible mouthing's.

"You said about us helping each other, well, what about Tom Reddie? He doesn't help anyone or even do anything," young David observed.

"No…that's true, but Tom is a special case."

Pondering the inequity of that, the boy challenged another disparity. "I tried to look in the computer before, some things about Earth, but it said 'no access,' and then some other words I didn't…"

"It would have said 'no access without authorization,'" Stratford recited. "That means you can't see in that area unless permitted to do so."

"Why not, though?"

"There are certain things the WSO felt we don't need to know. Even I can't access some information." He rubbed his son's shoulder in a gesture of parental sympathy. "Sorry, Son."

"But why can't we look? You're the captain."

"For one thing, in your case, it's because you're too young. And being Captain has nothing to do with it, because there are things I can't access, either.

I guess some information was kept from us for our own good; we just have to take it on faith that it's better we don't know."

"What's faith?"

*That's a tough one*, Stratford thought to himself. "It's a…faith is a belief in something that is based on our feelings about it, even in the absence of any facts to support our beliefs."

The child struggled with this concept for a moment. "How are you supposed to know if you're feeling is right?"

Stratford smiled in spite of himself: smart kid. "I guess that's where the faith part comes in. You simply have to believe it's right." He stood, bringing the discussion to a close for now. "Enough of this," he said firmly, and pointed David in the direction of his room. "Your mom should be back here shortly before we have to…" He left the sentence unfinished. The boy knew well enough where they had to go.

The phone rang just then, and the youngster eagerly grabbed it as he passed the computer heading toward his room. "Hi, Mom." Silence. "Dad's right here, do you want…Oh, we were just talking about stuff…the Mayflower…Almost…All I need to do is put on my shoes…No, we ate before…Okay, how long? I can tell him…okay, Mom. Bye."

Stratford's expectant look required an answer. "That was mom," he stated the obvious.

"Yes, she'll be here soon."

"No, she called to say she will have to meet us because she has to wait till Mrs. Breck gets there to relieve her."

Stratford checked the digital clock. "I think we better go now."

"Dad, I'm scared. I don't want to go to that room."

David had put on his shoes, and came next to his father, who knelt to give him a hug of reassurance. "Do you remember what I told you about that room?"

The child had buried his face into his father's shoulder, and looked up into his eyes. "Yes," he said, his voice muffled. "I'm still scared."

"David, there's absolutely nothing to be frightened of. I promise you."

"That's not what Mickey Woofter said."

*Another juvenile authority to contend with*, Stratford thought. "Okay, so what does Mickey say?"

"He said a little boy became dead there. It was Tom Reddie's brother, and Tom Reddie did it."

As Captain, Stratford sometimes found it necessary to distort the truth for reasons of expediency. As a father, he would not lie. "There was a terrible accident that happened," Stratford admitted. "That part is true, Son. Even still, there's no cause to be afraid. It's also true Tom Reddie did it. His brother's name was Allan, but it was an accident."

"Mickey said that's why Tom Reddie is crazy."

"David," Stratford reached under his son's chin and gently lifted his head. Father and son locked gazes. "I don't want you to ever use that word again about Tom...he's mentally disturbed. He indirectly caused his brother's death, and he's never gotten over it."

"Mentally 'sturbed?"

"Mentally disturbed...yes. It means he's suffered a terrible thing, and he can't face it because it hurts too much."

David gave careful consideration to this revelation. "Okay, Dad, I'm not afraid," he said in a show of bravado. "Long as you're there," he added.

# Chapter 21

The Mayflower contained a hospital facility, and logically, its antitheses. The funerary room was located beyond a partition of the auditorium. Upon entering, one noticed the thick-glassed display/evacuation tube that ran the length of the farthest end of the room. In keeping with its purpose, the lighting was subdued and sourced from the edge of the overhead, casting most objects into partial shadows. All designed to instill a melancholy of spirit. Decorative motifs were innocuous and secular, which suited the multicultural makeup of the crew. While some parameters used by Hardin to select volunteers for the Project appeared to factor out religious beliefs, it was more by accident than planned. These people honored science, and it was at an altar of physical laws they placed their faith.

Captain Stratford and David entered the funerary room and were greeted by George Cody. His profession was primarily as barber/beautician, but he also served as mortician and funeral director, which was thankfully an infrequent but essential calling.

He happened to be good at it too. Stratford had observed his comfortable manner during the memorial service held prior to the last shift. He hardly broke his rhythmic pace as he accommodated late arrivals, placing them like sentries along the bulkheads, while simultaneously dispensing good will.

This was the actual funeral service, and no less a gathering was now expected. Stratford's cursory inventory of the room confirmed the presence of the ship's officers and their families. There were the Lesters, Albert Breck and family, too, although his wife was on duty at the hospital. Scattered throughout the gathering, there was also the daSilvas, the Phens, and the Woofters. Each family patriarch gave a polite nod to their Captain when his eyes met theirs.

Lydia Stratford was seated near and to the left of the evacuation tube, and the Captain guided young David into the pair of seats to her right. Lydia greeted them by grasping the Captain's and David's hand in turn. "I was beginning to think you'd gotten lost," she whispered and forced a smile.

Stratford returned a tight-lipped smile. He was visibly ill at ease in contrast to Lydia's calm dignity. "I can't imagine where Halsey is," he whispered hoarsely. "Maybe I better tell Cody to begin." He approached the funeral director and engaged him in a subtle exchange of words. Stratford supplied most of them while Cody contributed the punctuation, occasional nods of affirmation or disagreement.

The door to the funerary room had been kept open. As Cody glanced into the auditorium, he decided no others would likely be forthcoming and signaled his assistant who responded on cue by dimming the lights. He escorted the Captain back to his seat and then mounted the short steps to ceremoniously take his place at the podium.

Having drawn the attention of the gathering, the room grew quieter as he issued a second furtive command. Now, the low register strains of music rose above and out of the silence. By degrees, the sound increased in volume from a single sustained note before erupting in a musical passage signifying a resigned farewell:

*There you stood on the edge of your feather – expecting to fly.*
*While I laughed, I wondered whether I could wave goodbye?*
*Knowing that you'd gone.*

"Sorry I'm late, David," a voice whispered in Stratford's ear, breaking into his private contemplations. "We fell a little behind." It was Halsey.

Young David relinquished the chair next to his father upon his mother's arrival. While standing, he lost his footing and slid, nearly tumbling. Halsey deftly caught hold of him at his elbow. "Mommy, I went Surfin' USA, huh?" he declared comically at his own expense, garnering an appreciative laughter from those nearby, even George Cody. He was referring to the recent dance craze that had swept the ship's youth, based on young John Morrison's discovery that the ship's computer could be used to edit material from their digital archives. Calling the system Interactive Karaoke, he was first successful at removing Beach Boy Mike Love from a video of the group playing their hit song on a soundstage and inserted himself in his place. Soon, all the young people became enamored of his invention, and they began staging Interactive Karaoke dances.

*If everybody had an ocean – 'cross the U.S.A.*
*Then everybody'd be surfin' like Californ-i-a.*

The first generation of Mayfloridians found it somewhat spooky. These children pretending to 'surf' in deepest space, having no idea what surfing even was. The kids, however, loved it.

The room grew ever more silent as the music ended. All faces turned toward Cody, and he pointedly cleared his throat once, then twice. "Colonel David S. Stratford," he began, pausing for breath as much for affect. "Our Captain of the Mayflower these first twenty-eight years was also a devoted husband, loving father, and grandfather." Nearly everyone shifted their gaze toward Lydia and her small family. "We also counted him as part of the extended family of the Mayflower Project, and he was also our friend."

Lydia claimed the deepest memories and suffering at his loss. She raised her eyes and looked at his elaborately wrapped body as it rested in the glass evacuation tube before them. There was small comfort, at least, in that he passed peacefully and quickly. She was grateful for that, except it left no opportunity for goodbyes.

She had awakened three days, shifts, earlier to a strange foreboding that something was wrong. She reached over to touch his face. He was lying cold and pale beside her, but she already knew. Later, she recalled how different, tired and worn-out, he had become. He was, after all, seventy years old. It occurred to her: would things have been different if they had never left Earth? Would he still be alive? They were only marginally younger (according to Einstein) traveling out here at 240,000 miles per hour. How much difference could it have made?

She forced herself to look again upon his body. Who expects to live forever? He did, Colonel David S. Stratford. Well, he wanted a kind of immortality, which in a way, was like living forever. "Lesser men are doomed to procreate while greatness itself is borne of creation," he had said. His life was as close to that ideal as anyone ever gets, she decided.

Cody had continued his eulogy. "He held an honorable goal," he was saying. "Not only for himself, but for all others aboard this ship. That goal is now ours to fulfill…ours to instill dedication in the generations to come and complete this mission entrusted to us by the citizens of planet Earth." When it became obvious that Cody had reached the close of his address, he received an enthusiastic, if not heartfelt applause. He summoned to the stage the newly appointed Captain Stratford, generation 2, who rose and took his place at the podium while the funeral director receded into the shadowy background.

The gathering looked into the eyes of this second Mayflower Captain trustingly and with a feeling that amounted to pride, especially in his mother, Lydia. There was much of the father about him, and it was more than his appearance, although they did share certain features: the full hairline, for instance. Mainly, David inherited certain personality traits, such as his father's sense of duty and confidence, which would prove essential to the task he had been raised, no, bred to do.

"For our family," he spoke quietly but with enough volume to be heard, "we'd like to thank George for the wonderful eulogy he gave my father. Also, we thank everyone for your show of sympathy. As he often said, he believed in the scientific worth of the Project, which even death cannot alter or defile. Ultimately, death gives us impetus toward its conclusion."

He then began to relate a story told to him by his father. The Stratford family had been long settled in Adams County, Ohio, and their farm was a mere few miles from the famous Serpent Mound, a favorite site of exploration for him as a boy. The indigenous people of Brush Creek Valley had built the earthen structure around 1000 B.C. in the shape of a writhing snake that appeared to be swallowing an egg. Once thought to be a burial site, it likely had a deeper, spiritual significance, perhaps as a means to commune with their spiritual world or as a metaphor for the ancient asteroid that had impacted near the site: 'Earth swallows satellite' represented as 'snake swallows egg.'

"My father was less interested in what its architects had in mind by building it. He was more concerned by what was in the hearts of the laborers who struggled for their own private reasons," David Stratford said. "Perhaps, it was to enshrine a part of themselves, proclaiming in the face of mortality: 'I was here.' But given enough time, the mound erodes and buildings fall, making all human endeavors finite."

His voice brimmed with passion as he laid bare his father's thoughts and words. He leaned over the podium slightly, taking in the faces before him and gauged their reactions. "We represent that attempt by our kind to conquer mortality. My father believed the Mayflower Project was the final apotheosis of mankind, succeeding in the defeat of time and space, whereby our collective effort would be heard as one voice saying: 'We existed.'"

David relaxed now, but before he turned to leave the podium, the entire gathering erupted in applause. Many of those present, including his wife Halsey, were in tears. The young captain was stunned, preventing him from speaking further.

George Cody allowed their enthusiasm to run its course unabated before stepping forward to announce the conclusion of the ceremony. "I don't think anyone, including Colonel Stratford himself, could have said that better," he declared and shook David's hand in a show of admiration. There was a very brief smattering of applause, but it was withdrawn quickly when Cody held up a hand. "In memory and consolation, this concludes the celebration for the life of our fallen Captain. The family requests time now for their private contemplations. So, if you would, everybody, please exit starting front rows to back."

Halsey and her young son left their seats to join David by the podium while Lydia remained, her gaze fixed on the wrapped body of her late husband. "That was beautiful, honey." Halsey said softly in his ear.

David smiled sadly but didn't respond. He reached down and scooped up his son and carried him to the evacuation tube as Halsey followed. "Should I say goodbye to Grandpa now?" the child asked quizzically and looked at each parent in turn.

Stratford put him down. "I guess so, little buddy. You better say goodbye."

The boy stood close to the tube, his breath causing a patch of condensation to appear as he contemplated the body within. He brought his hands close to his mouth, as if passing along a secret. "Goodbye, Grandpa," he said in a barely audible voice. "I'm sorry you're dead. If you can hear me, I love you."

David and Halsey were both touched by their son's display and drew close behind him. While the boy was fond of Brian Lester, Halsey's father, and his maternal grandfather, he had a special bond with Captain Stratford.

"So, I can't see him anymore because he's dead?" he asked, less for the answer than the need to be convinced it was true.

"Yes, I explained that. None of us can see him after this," David explained patiently. "But inside of you, you'll remember him, and it will be like he's always with you...right here." He tapped his son playfully on top of his head.

"And why can't we go see him?"

"Because we would die if we went outside. Do you remember the story I was telling you about Tom Reddie and his brother Allan?"

"Yes."

"Well, the first person to die aboard ship was Thomas Reddie, the Mayflower's original navigator. I was only eight or nine years old, and his twin sons were about my age."

"They were your friends, Dad?"

"Yes, they were. Just like you and Mickey Woofter. But this is what happened: They missed their father so much they decided after the funeral for one of them to leave the ship and bring him back."

"That's how Allan died? He went outside?"

"Yes, Son. The boys didn't understand that we're safe only in here, inside the Mayflower. There's no air outside, and it's also very cold."

"Tom Reddie is…acts like he does because of what happened to Allan?"

"Well, he feels responsible because he operated the system," and David pointed at the set of switches mounted several feet away beneath the rolled edge of the tube. "It was designed so it couldn't be operated alone, which could prevent someone from committing…taking their own life. So, Allan went in the tube. Afterward, Tom waited for his brother and father, and when they didn't return, he panicked, realizing what he had done. He had stayed hidden in here for days, listening at the bulkhead for Allan to come back while everyone searched the entire ship for them. Grandpa Stratford was the one who found him in here. At first, Tom refused to leave. He was so afraid he'd miss Allan's signal. He's been like that ever since – the way he behaves – because he felt responsible for Allan's death."

"He's sad because of Allan?"

"Yes. He was too young to be blamed for what happened, and no one did, of course. But he feels responsible. He lost his father, then his brother, and a few years ago, his mother died, too."

"That's too bad. He's all alone. I feel sorry for Tom."

"We all do. That's why no one bothers him. We let him live quietly in his cabin; his meals are taken to him. No one expects anything of him."

George Cody had stepped out earlier, but he returned. He approached David. "Will you be wanting me to stay here awhile?" He looked significantly at the evacuation tube and back at David, who understood his meaning.

"Well, let me ask my mother what she wants." He then turned to Halsey. "Dear, why don't you take David and go to our cabin. I'll attend to what needs to be done here, and I'll be along later."

"Okay," she agreed, and grabbed a quick kiss. She approached Lydia with David in tow. "Mom, I'll see you soon," she said, embracing Lydia.

"Bye, Grandma," the boy said as he grabbed a quick hug. "I love you even more to help make you happy again."

"And I'll love you back just as much," Lydia vowed, closing her eyes and holding him close. "Grandpa loves you, too."

David turned away to look at his grandfather, knowing it was for the last time. "Bye forever, Grandpa. I won't forget you always. I promise."

Lydia decided she needed to be left alone for a while. "I'll be fine. I just want some time with David," she said over her son's protests.

"Do you...do either of you want me to come back later..." Cody asked hesitantly. "Do you think you'll need me...I don't mind, you know, if either of you can't..."

Both Lydia and her son knew what he meant – triggering the mechanism. Granted, it was a weird visual, the Captain's body, wrapped like a chrysalis, rushing out the evacuation tube and careening through space.

"Mom, it's up to you. If you want, either George or I can come back later," David said, looking at his mother expectantly. "What do you think?"

# Chapter 22

Lydia was stronger than either of them imagined. She was also still very much an Earthling, a 20th century Earthling. It occurred to her: should a son by necessity have to "bury" his father, even by the push of button, tossing him effortlessly into frozen space? She recalled John-John Kennedy's poignant salute as his slain father's coffin passed. Were the rules of duty or protocol different being born in space as her son was?

"I appreciate that, both of you," she said finally, and reached for her son's hand. "I really don't know yet. But if I find, I can't…" She left the sentence open-ended. "George, for all of us, we appreciate everything you did…the words and your effort meant a great deal to me and my family."

Cody nodded; his lips tight. "That's okay. David was a great Captain, but more than that, he was also a good friend. I only hope I did him justice." When Lydia and David assured him that he had, Cody laughed dismissively. "Fair enough. Say no more. I can only wish when I'm gone someone will be able to work up a few nice things to say about me."

He gestured for them to follow as he proceeded to the control panel to demonstrate the system's simple operation. Cody first locked it down, securing the air-tight seal which would hold enough air under pressure to force the evacuation of the Captain's body. "When you're ready, just flip this cover to one side – like this," he said, revealing two switches beneath. "The yellow one primes the system, and it's pressed first," he explained. "The red one effects the evacuation."

Lydia watched carefully but again emphasized her desire to be alone, and both her son and George Cody departed, each of them promising to return if summoned. She settled wearily into the nearest chair and quietly contemplated the shared life she had made with her husband. It was strange. Most of what she found herself reminiscing about took place pre-Mayflower; but then, the Project had been David's passion. However, David had been hers. She finally realized that he was gone. There was measurably less pleasure in being a part of it.

Lydia became vaguely conscious that a shadow had fallen along the wall just beyond her peripheral vision; it angled down and passed over the evacuation tube and onto the floor. Accompanied by a shuffling sound, by now she realized with a start she was not alone.

It was Tom Reddie.

"Mrs. Stratford, I'm very sorry if I scared you," he apologized in a hollow-sounding voice. His voice sounded unused and out of practice.

While Tom's sudden appearance surprised Lydia as much as frightened her, she looked into his eyes and saw only a passive honesty. He was incapable of deception. It had been many years since she had spoken to him and couldn't recall the last time he had even been in her presence. Probably, not since the accident, even though her own son had been close to the Reddie twins.

"No, Tom. I only thought…I thought I was alone. I'm pleased to see you, though. I'm guessing you came to see the Captain?"

He answered indirectly but offered an explanation. "Captain Stratford had always been nice to me…even that time he found me. He was nice to my mother, too. He used to come to our cabin and talk to us. Then later, he'd come talk to…just me."

She never knew that. David had never mentioned it. "He would have appreciated you coming to see him now, Tom. I'm glad you did."

He glanced timidly around the funerary room. Gathering resolve, he stepped nearer to view the wrapped body of Captain Stratford. "It's been a long time," he said quietly as he stared inside the tube. "A long time since I've been in this room."

Lydia found it difficult to find something innocuous to say. "I think it's good that you came then, Tom. Sometimes it's best to face our fears," she offered. "But tell me: what sort of things did you and the Captain talk about?"

Tom brightened at the memories the question invoked. "Oh, there were so many. One of my favorite things was when he told me about Earth."

"What did he say about it?"

"Well, he said it was a lot like the garden. The color of the plants was like the color of the Earth; everything was green and beautiful." He turned and smiled at Lydia as he reflected on what he had seen or just imagined. "It sounded like a wonderful place. You know, sometimes I've wondered, Mrs.

Stratford. Maybe, when we die, we go to a beautiful place. Do you think it's true? Maybe, we'll go to Earth. Maybe, my family is waiting there," he said dreamily. "I'd like that to be true, anyway."

Lydia didn't comment, figuring Tom's vision of the hereafter was hardly more or less absurd than anyone's. Perhaps death was…pleasant. Maybe, it's about choices; you'll actually have a say in where you spend your eternity. David had always been noncommittal about the subject. He never speculated openly or even appeared concerned about it. He would likely be quite content to drift amongst the stars in his own very private eternity.

It was at this moment that Lydia realized she was emotionally incapable of effecting the dumping of her husband's body into space. Perhaps, it was the sense of finality or the ghastly visual. She didn't know, but did know, nonetheless, there was no way she could bring herself to do it. No way. She stood and began walking past Tom Reddie.

"What is it, Mrs. Stratford?" he asked. "Are you leaving now?"

"No, I'm not. It's okay," she affirmed quickly, as she tried to avoid looking at the control panel. "I'm not leaving. I just realized I can't…do that. I'm going to have to call George Cody. I thought at first I'd be able…but I can't."

"I'll do it, Mrs. Stratford," Tom volunteered. "There's no need for Mr. Cody. I can do it."

"Are you sure?" she asked tentatively. "I mean, you don't have to. I wouldn't want you to feel…uncomfortable…"

Tom shook his head emphatically. "No, I don't mind. I'm glad to help you. And if it's the last kind thing I can do for Captain Stratford, I'm glad to help him."

"You really thought highly of him, didn't you?"

"Yes, I did. He took the time to try and talk to me and make me feel better after what happened to my brother. He said it wasn't my fault. Being a part of the Mayflower Project meant Allan would still be alive, he said. Maybe it means we all will be immortal. Do you think that's true?"

Immortality. The Mayflower Project. Lydia began to weep, uncontrollably, and she hardly knew why.

# Part Two: Interlude

# Chapter 23

It was a balmy day in south Florida. A gentle breeze swept inland across the Atlantic and cooled the pavement outside. NASA's chief finance officer, Alex Bentz, strode through the remnants of previous missions in what now looked like an eerie graveyard of twisted metal and debris rather than priceless relics from missions past that marked man's quests beyond Earth. Last weeks' category 4 hurricane had plowed through Cape Canaveral's aerospace exhibits like a runway freight train, and as he surveyed the damage, Alex dreaded being the person in charge of selectively choosing which were to be repaired and which recycled.

"Damn insurance adjusters and government bureaucrats…too cheap to ensure the remembrance of these milestones…and I'm left to decide which ones deserve an allocation from the menial budget available for repairs…I've never heard of most of these missions."

The year was 7779, and in the last millennia, man had abandoned their futile quest to conquer the stars. It was now assumed that, yes, indeed, life was bound to exist beyond Earth, but travels to any of these places unrealistic, impossible, and beyond reach. Instead, the aerospace industry shifted focus to within our own solar system. In fact, we had colonized numerous planets, moons, and even bodies within the Kyper Belt.

Alex gazed at an undiscernible, twisted relic of one of some mission and tried to make out the inscription on the bronze remains. He reached for his glasses. As he put them on, he heard someone's approach. He turned to find a young, eager-looking boy approaching. Alex turned to the boy and asked, "Greetings, anyway you can help me out over here? I'm trying to read this plaque and can't seem to decipher it. The hurricane really did a number on this one."

*The boy approached Alex, and in his flight suit*, Alex thought, "this is fantastic…a pilot…maybe he'll know what's what."

The boy squinted at the plaque, "Mayflower Project, Colonel David Stratford…Huh…never heard of him."

Alex replied, "With its weight, it will fetch about $90,000 at the recycling center. Bronze prices are low right now, but I've never heard of this mission either. It will cost a fortune to repair." He glanced at his clipboard and located the statue on his spreadsheet. Without hesitation, he checked the box for recycle.

As he finished his work, Alex repeated wondered about this David Stratford. Who was he and why did his name sound so familiar?

# Part Three: Conclude

# Chapter 24

Michael Woofter had been sorting through several handfuls of file disks, seated at the desk in the garden's office. He snapped his head suddenly, as if to catch a prankster in the act, because he was certain the lights had dimmed slightly. This was the end of his shift, and being simultaneously tired and even bored, he just wondered if he imagined it. Malfunctions of any kind were rare, as the Mayflower was kept to a rigid maintenance schedule.

He returned to his task warily, and it happened again. This time there was no mistake. Looking overhead, he squinted slightly, observing the four sets of two lighting units in the ceiling. He turned to gaze through the glass into the garden complex beyond, confirming those lights were alternately brightening and dimming. Then, as he watched, and to his considerable surprise, all the lights extinguished altogether.

He dropped the disks in disgust onto the desktop, producing a muffled clattering. "Ain't this a bitch, McMurphy!" Michael exclaimed, using his pet catch phrase. Caught off-guard with the novelty of a systems failure, he was quite unprepared. *Should he first examine the emergency procedures manual on the computer?* he thought. Good idea, except there's no power, he berated himself. It also occurred to him that the auxiliary power lamps in the recesses of the bulkheads had failed to activate. After a few moments, it appeared they had no intention of doing so. He considered the potential ramifications. Had this problem affected other areas of the Mayflower? A glimmer of panic crept into Michael's brain stem and snapped into his cortex.

As his eyes adjusted to the darkness, he noticed a light flashing on the garden's large control panel. It was the automatic emergency indicator, and he relaxed now, knowing the alert was being spread the length and breadth of the ship. This system operated on an independent circuit, and Michael knew that because only one light was flashing. The problem was isolated to the garden.

There was nothing to do but wait for the maintenance detail which should arrive shortly.

Feeling compelled to do something…anything…he carefully navigated his way to the door that led to the main concourse. Grasping the manual release handle, he by-passed the now useless entry pad and forced the heavy panel open. In contrast to the blackened office, the well-lit concourse caused him to blink, but he still could recognize Charles Perry and his son walking casually toward him. Both were laden with substantial tool kits. Given the circumstances of a power failure of this magnitude in Michael's garden, their lackadaisical pace irritated him.

"We don't have to guess we're in the right place, Michael," the elder Perry observed in a friendly tone. "Can you tell how bad it is?"

"I have absolutely no idea," Michael's reply dripped sarcasm. "I think that's your department. All I can tell you is it seems like all the power is out. I can't hear any of the equipment running in the garden, anyway."

Perry peered into the open doorway. "There's no emergency power either, huh?"

"Maybe you can tell me," the gardener challenged.

"I guess not," Perry said flatly. "Hey, listen, Michael. I didn't cause this outage, and we're here to fix it not for your abuse, so you can stuff your…"

"Yes, I understand, Charles. I know it's not your fault, I know. I'm actually…it's just that I'm concerned about the plants, that's all. We have a carefully worked out schedule for light exposure, feeding, and watering, and I'm afraid this down time could be disruptive. I'm really sorry I jumped on you. It's not your fault," the gardener sputtered an apology.

"Oh, hell, Michael, forget it," Charles said affably.

"I know it's not healthy to think about it, but something like this makes me wonder what would happen if all the ships' systems went down, and we couldn't set them right again," Michael said as he glanced knowingly toward an outer bulkhead. His skin prickled at the thought of it.

"I guess in that case we'd all be dead," Charles said matter-of-factly. "But that's okay…just forget it." The electrician shifted the weight of his tool kit. "I may not understand your work here, Woofter, but we all like to eat," he teased. "Besides, we'll both be glad for something to do that's interesting. Anything. Seems like we spend most of our time in our work shack just recharging battery packs or rebuilding circuit boxes or light bulbs. I can't remember the last time we had a serious call. Chuckie," he asked his son, "Do you? When was it? Ten, maybe eleven shifts ago?"

"I'm not sure, Dad. Seems like at least that many."

"Well, I can't say that I, or likely any of the Mayflower's crew, shares your enthusiasm for system failures, large or small," Michael protested. "I think we'd all feel safest if…"

"You know, Chuckie, it was that many shifts," Perry suddenly recalled, "It was in the kitchen. A whole bunch of microwave ovens went down. Remember?"

"Yes, that's it," the younger Perry agreed.

"No one missed a meal, either," Charles avowed. "So, don't worry. We ain't about to let your – correction, our plants die."

Michael recognized that Charles Perry's consistently optimistic demeanor could be mistaken for incompetence and was greatly relieved in the knowledge it wasn't true. While rarely discussed, everyone aboard shared a kind of primordial fear about the viability of the Mayflower residing at an instinctual level. This had been true of generation 1, while 16,130 years into the Project, at generation 216, these inheritors were no exception.

The gardener remained standing at the doorway as the Perrys' passed within the office, as if coaxing light to gather therein. The electricians proceeded to the air-lock door, which led into the garden itself.

"Michael, I'm leaving you this extra flashlight," Perry advised as he placed the item on the desk. "We'll need you at these controls as we test the system."

# Chapter 25

Woofter secured the door open and obediently took his seat to await further instructions, while he watched the maintenance team enter the garden. He marked their progress by observing the swath made by the back-and-forth motion of their flashlights. It was eerily reflective in the high humidity of the garden's atmosphere.

The power grid system they were seeking was accessible but housed separately from the garden itself. Taken largely for granted until now, its intricacies had only garnered a cursory interest from Woofter. Now he realized, it enabled the growing of the ship's food supply under these most unnatural of conditions.

The flashlight Charles had left for Michael afforded him little comfort, so he simply sat and waited for the technicians to do their job. The Perrys' wizardry manifested itself quickly, as Michael detected the auxiliary lighting begin to emit a soft yellow-orange glow. Almost simultaneously, as if choreographed, Charles's voice erupted from the intercom. "Woofter, are you reading me? You should have the emergency lights. Acknowledge, please. Over."

"I read you, Charles," Michael responded excitedly. "The emergency power is on but weak. Repeat. Emergency power is affirmative but weak. Over." He glanced at the nearest light in gratitude. While Michael watched, the lights grew brighter by degrees.

"It should look better now, but I think this is going to be more than we bargained for, so be patient, Michael. You're only going to have auxiliary capacity for a while. Over."

Another voice spoke to the gardener. It did not emanate from the speaker in front of him, but from the doorway. Looking over, he saw David Stratford, Captain of the Mayflower." I saw your power was down," Stratford explained. "I wanted to see for myself how bad it was."

"We really don't know yet, "Michael replied. "The Perrys just got here. So far, they have the auxiliary on," and he pointed at the lights that still glowed softly along the walls.

"That's it so far. You don't know what they found out there?"

Michael was impressed with the Captain's concern and response. "We were in a total blackout at first. He did say it might be more involved than he first thought."

"Well, very good," Stratford enthused. "Charles knows his job. I'm sure he'll put it right again." The Captain had entered the office and glanced at the control panel layout over Michael's shoulder. "Ask him if there's anything he needs from me."

Michael pressed the speaker intercom button. "Charles, Captain Stratford is here. He wants to know if he can help in anyway. Over."

"No. In fact, I'm leaving Chuck out here, and I'm coming back to the office. Tell the Captain to stay put, though. I have something interesting to show you both. Over and out."

# Chapter 26

The elder Perry re-entered the office moments later, carrying a thoroughly soaked piece of electrical hardware. He placed it noisily at Michael's feet, forming a puddle of water. "Hello, Captain," he nodded. "Corrosion," he announced by way of explaining the box, as if the one word was sufficient.

"Yeah, I see. Corrosion," Michael repeated blankly. "But how exactly do you mean that?"

"It's corroded," the electrician repeated testily, as if explaining to a dull-witted child. "And there's at least two more out there that are almost as bad as this one. It's the moisture in there that's doing it."

Michael couldn't help but feel that Charles seemed to hold him personally to blame for the corrosive action of the garden's water but thought better than raise a protest.

"Can it be repaired, Charles?" Stratford asked.

"Oh, sure. See these little hashmarks on the inside of the casing here?" Perry knelt and shone his light on the box. "Each one of these represent when the unit was rebuilt."

The Captain and Michael looked on in amazement. There were at least a hundred such marks.

"I don't recognize all of them, but these crescent-shaped ones belong to my grandfather and father, for sure."

"That's amazing," Stratford said. "They're easily repaired, I take it – recycled over and over."

"These junction boxes contain thousands of micro-circuits that can drive your entire operation out there," Perry lectured, and jerked a thumb toward the garden. "In other applications, they can run the kitchen, or media center, or whatever you need."

"And a little water ruins…," Michael began.

"A little water?" Perry said sarcastically. "It's drenched. Despite all the protective coatings of silicon, the garden stays so wet the water just seeps through. You can't stop it. That's what caused your main system and the feedback loop to the auxiliary backup to fail." He held the box up and looked it over contemplatively. "But on the plus side, we have all the replacement parts we need in our shack, so it's only a matter of wiring them in."

"Won't we run out of parts eventually?" Michael asked.

"No, even the parts themselves can be rebuilt. We don't throw away nothin'."

"How's that done?"

"Those mini-circuits I remove can be rebuilt, remanufactured, actually. It's hard to explain how it's done, but basically, we melt them down. My ancestral father was the first director of maintenance," he added proudly. "He was the first to develop the technique of recasting the circuits and fusing it to metal substrate, which makes repairing this equipment over and over possible. How about that?"

"That is fascinating, Charles," Michael said. "I also recall it was your ancestral parents who bore the first Mayflower child. My ancestral father designed the garden complex," he added. "Do either of you know how he came to be aboard the Mayflower?"

Both Captain Stratford and Charles Perry admitted they didn't know the story.

"Well, both he and my ancestral mother were taken as crew members at the last moment before the Mayflower left Earth's orbit as replacements for another scientist who actually went insane and tried to sabotage the ship."

"Insane?" asked Stratford, somewhat incredulously. "But didn't they realize that before he was chosen to be a member of the Project?"

"Well, I don't know," Michael said, shrugging. "I agree it makes no sense, Captain, but that's the legend. It's part of the historical record, if you ever want to look at it, it's all there."

"Have you read it?" Charles asked.

"Yes, I have. I've read it a few times, as a matter of fact. It made me wonder how things would have been different because…"

"Things? What things?" the electrician interrupted.

"Us. I mean…what if that substitution hadn't taken place? Who would I be or would I even exist? Who would any of us be, for that matter? Would we be completely different or only slightly different? A small change in the gene pool could have produced major consequences…" his voice trailed off.

His companions failed to grasp Michael's argument. They were unmoved.

"You're too much for me, Michael," Perry laughed dismissively. "Why worry about something like that? Things are as they are, and that's good enough for me."

Ever the diplomat, Stratford withheld comment. Had he expressed his sentiments they would have mirrored Perry's.

"You know, Michael, it's like that song: 'I am he, as you are he, as you are me, and we are all together.' That's all you'll ever need to know."

Perry's comments and Stratford's silence effectively halted any further debate, and so Michael fell silent.

While this namesake of the ancestral Michael Woofter could be construed as high-handed as the original, he did realize Charles Perry had a point. With the Project only half completed, more or less, it was futile to agonize over one's circumstance or the place and time you were born into. As Charles said, they were "all together," and each person shared bloodlines uniting them that could be traced to each of the first families. As a result, any racial or ethnic distinctions had long ago faded, only to be replaced by specimens who were neither red nor yellow or black or white. Even though the WSO had supplied them with enough frozen egg and sperm for those circumstances when natural conception was impossible or to introduce new blood lines, any departure from standard failed to persist for long.

In mathematical terms, everything tends toward the mean. However, that is not to say these inheritors of the Mayflower Project were "average." On the contrary, it was to the WSO's credit they could engineer over the course of a 33,201-year mission a race of progenitors that remained consistent and committed. The analysis of genealogical data insured their health and viability by introducing new seed at regular intervals to season the human "soup."

Michael Woofter 216 represented a pronounced skew to the bell-shaped Mayflower norm, and his departure from standard issue amounted to more than his lighter skin tone and eyes of cobalt blue. He was more emotional and volatile, and a geneticist might have described him as a 'sport.' His maternal grandfather's essence whose identity was unofficially unknown had been kept at −200°C for these 16,100 years. Ostensibly, he was the cause of Michael's unusual variance.

His wife Jamie shared a similar circumstance. In her case, the paternal grandfather was the source of new blood, making her family tree as different as Michael's.

From their earliest childhood, these two had been inseparable. As they grew older, their love deepened and matured; they eventually married. Their choice of professions was an extension of their romantic passions: both trained under Michael's father, Harmon, who was the former director of the garden. Having only recently stepped down, the elder Woofter had remained on staff as a laborer, albeit on a greatly reduced workload. This change had allowed Jamie to assume the position of second-in-command, an unusual circumstance, as husband-wife teams were seldom approved in any of the ship's departments. In light of the Woofter's recent notification by the maternity center they were to be scheduled to begin a family, it was not thought to be an impediment to their work if Jamie stayed in the job; they would have to work separate shifts once the baby arrived, anyway.

# Chapter 27

The intercom suddenly snapped to life. "Michael, this is Chuck Perry. Could you put my father on, please? Over."

The gardener shifted positions slightly to accommodate Charles, who had to reach around him to access the talk-back.

"Chuckie, what do you have? Over."

"It's like you thought, Dad. Two of these other circuit boxes tested dead and need rebuilt. I replaced some of the pressed boards with ones we had with us in a few other boxes, and those should be fine. I'm pulling these two to take back to the shack. I'm leaving here now, and I'll be up front shortly. Over and out."

By way of interpretation, Charles turned to his companions. "Well, you heard him. Looks like we'll have to do a few overhauls. No big deal. Luckily, we had enough parts to rebuild a few on site," he said confidently. "Not as bad as it looks, gentlemen."

"That's great," Michael said dubiously. "But Jamie is due to start her shift, and I still haven't completed the guide her group needs for the harvest."

"No problem. What we have to do shouldn't take too long. These circuit boxes are beautiful. There are thousands of them throughout the ship and they're identical. What they're used for determines how they work, but they are all generic. When we repair the ones that we pulled out of the garden, they'll end up in our inventory only to be used someplace else. See how it works? You gotta hand it to those engineers who designed this thing. They knew what the hell they were doing." Charles stopped his discourse for a moment when his son came in.

"Yeah, I realize," the gardener began, but Perry cut him off.

"It's a matter of hauling a few boxes down here and plugging them in." He snapped his fingers in Michael's face. Several times.

"Okay. Well, in that case, I guess the Perrys have things under control," Stratford absently made his excuses. "I have to attend to some other matters. I'll be in the control room if you need me. Let me now if there are any other problems here, Charles."

Michael resented that last statement. Despite the fact that Perry also served as second officer, he felt it should have been directed at him. No doubt the Perry's knew their jobs well, and the gardener respected that. But did they, Perry 216, anyway, know his place? The garden was Michael's domain, and if a problem arose there, Mayflower protocol dictated that Michael should report to the Captain. A trifling complaint, perhaps, but the facts were well represented: Stratford and Perry were friends. While not forbidden by any regulations, certainly, but Perry was the only person aboard that the Captain was ever known to defer to.

Michael's mood brightened considerably, however, once the power was restored full up, and he prepared to complete the crop assessments he had begun earlier. Donning his rain gear, he was splashed repeatedly as he entered the garden by thick water droplets spawned by the heavy mist. He stopped to engage the engines that rotated the crop platforms, then stepped aboard as the entire system creaked and groaned. It rose slowly, penetrating through the quilted green canopy, and he watched the other motionless platforms seem to recede away. Breathing deeply in the vastness of this living garden, the sights and smells enhanced Michael's sense of well-being. Yet, the strangely surreal notion of this garden being transported through lifeless space never occurred to him. Having no standard of comparison, it was without qualifications his beautiful world.

As the peak of rotation was reached, the mist became thick and opaque, and the dozens of artificial suns dispersed light into rainbows. Other platforms were accessible at this height by narrow catwalks, and Michael proceeded to inspect the plants he had earlier believed ready for harvest. Corn, squash, spinach, tomatoes, and strawberries were fully ripe and duly noted. The waxy yellow shells of the butternut squash were especially prized but not as food. Instead, John Friesen, who ran the manufacturing section, would process them into paper. Michael also observed that the cotton had burst forth from their bolls, which was also used to produce various necessities.

The secret to producing the large yields they required was only partly due to the physical work involved. It was the planning. Specifically, the WSO's planning, as the plants sent along with the first generation were already nearly mutant in size. They had brought the best varieties available many of them developed by Michael Woofter 1, and each successive generation had gradually improved upon them. The strawberries were, on average, as large as a man's fist.

As he completed his work, Michael detected above the drone of the garden's normal cacophony three throaty blasts from the horn used to signal someone in the garden from the office. Looking over the edge of the catwalk he knew already he'd see his father: three blasts was Harmon's signal. Jamie used two while Michael used one.

"Did you complete the evaluation?" Harmon shouted as Michael descended to the garden floor and stepped off. "I heard there was a power failure out here. What the hell happened?"

Michael held out an index finger and pointed at the office. "Let's get out of here first," he said loudly.

Both men passed through the first air-lock while Michael closed it securely behind them. They removed their outer wear and then went into the office.

"So, what happened, Michael?" his father asked once they were seated.

Michael shrugged. "One minute I was sitting at the console here, and then, the power failed. Perry said it was caused by corrosion. I can tell you this, it knocked out everything, including the emergency system."

"Did it put you very far behind with planning the harvest?"

"No, I was almost done when it happened. I had to verify my estimates, but I still haven't logged them into the computer. Overall, though, I guess it didn't hurt us too badly."

"Good news, then." Harmon agreed. "I assume they corrected the whole thing. This isn't going to happen again, is it?"

"I'm sure they did," Michael said, then gave out a laugh. "Charles said they guaranteed their work. He assured me it should last for two generations, at least."

"Fair enough. It'll be someone else's worry by then," Harmon observed. "So, tell me: what's the assignment going to be, chief?" he asked jokingly.

"Let's save it until Jamie and the others arrive," Michael advised.

# Chapter 28

The garden detail was considered the best alternative work on the Mayflower, and nearly everyone volunteered, being the only place aboard that provided a change in scenery. Even those not assigned to work often came into the office during their leisure time on some pretense, just to press their faces against the windows and marvel at the lush world within.

The doorway snapped quickly open, admitting Jamie Woofter and Wendy Breck, who seemed to have concluded a lively conversation just as they entered the office. Jamie flashed a smile at Michael who reciprocated in kind. She also nodded cheerily to Harmon. In a brief moment, the door opened again, and this time, Steve Lester and Martin Collins entered, completing the team for the harvest.

"Okay, everyone," Michael began, and all faces turned toward his. "I guess we'll get started. I'm sure you all know about the power outage, but as you can see, we're on full power now – courtesy of the talented Mr. Charles Perry and son," which elicited a gentle pattering of hands. "Despite this small set back, we will still be on schedule."

Michael continued speaking, outlining the specifics of the harvest. Jamie would document the proceedings, while Harmon would guide the others in the physical work. Both Steve Lester and Martin Collins were normally in maintenance/housekeeping, while Wendy Breck was a nurse. This system of multi-tasking, so eloquently conceived by the WSO, was still viable even some 16,000 years into the Project. It allowed more tasks to be performed by less people, keeping the population at an optimum level and keeping morale high.

When Michael finished, Harmon led the workers into the garden. Jamie stayed behind with her husband, as her role was to document the proceedings. After the others left, it was the couple's first opportunity to share an embrace.

"Guess what?" Jamie asked playfully, her arms around Michael's neck. She bit her lower lip, suppressing a smile.

"Well...let's see," Michael said blankly. "I couldn't begin to guess."

"You give up too easy. Try."

"Okay...I, ah...I don't know. I really don't. How about a hint?"

"Michael, let me have some fun, will you?" Jamie pretended to be angry. "Just think about it."

"I might think it had something to do with Wendy. When you came in, you seemed to be having a nice conversation with her. Does it have anything to do with Wendy?"

"Maybe," she toyed with her husband, "and maybe not. Didn't you understand? I told you you'll have to guess, but I'll give you just one hint: I received a phone call just before I came on duty."

The clue fairly gave it away now, and a huge smile broke out on Michael's face. The game was worth the wait. There was only one call they had been waiting for. "You heard from Audrey Lester, right?"

Jamie clasped her hands tightly around Michael's neck and pulled him close. "Yes, my dear. She wanted me to check with you, and we're to call her back and set up an appointment," Jamie said brightly.

"Is that all? She didn't say anything else?"

"No, I don't think she wanted to get into any specifics with just me. I think she prefers to speak to both of us at the same time."

"That's fine. I'll set it up after your shift. Once this harvest is done, we both have some down time for a while." Michael indicated the seat next to him. "Speaking of which, let's go over these other details. With the power failure, I never got a chance to log in."

"What about crop rotations?" Jamie inquired.

"They're done. The main thing is to remember to sort out the overripe stuff and have Martin or Steve extract the seeds. John Friesen will be sending his people for the cotton, but tell him to pick up the squash shells from the kitchen." Michael rested his hand on Jamie's. "It's all yours."

"I'll see you shortly, then," Jamie answered as she moved over to Michael's vacated seat. "Remember to call Audrey..."

"Yes, I will call Audrey," Michael repeated his instructions. "I'm going to stop at media on the way to the cabin and maybe order a movie."

"Well, certainly if you can find time for a movie, you should find time to call Audrey," Jamie lectured.

"Sure, no problem. That's one commodity we never run out of aboard Mother Mayflower – time." Michael tossed off sarcastically.

# Chapter 29

"*Casablanca*? Sure, that's a good movie, but somehow, I've always disliked the ending to that one. But to each his own," John Morrison said authoritatively. Michael had stopped at the media center to request a movie and was pleased to find John Morrison on duty. Despite his bombastic personality, he was very knowledgeable regarding the Mayflower's film library, and Michael regularly attended the seminars Morrison presented in the auditorium. Not surprisingly, nearly every inhabitant of the Mayflower – from generation 1 to the present – was a dedicated movie fan. While there were other forms of entertainment, those treasured films were a means to vicariously experience other worlds, thereby maturing as citizens in a world of supreme restrictions.

"Really? I can't say I agree; it's always been a favorite of mine, including the ending," Michael countered defensively. "But I'm interested. What's your objection to it?"

"I think they simply got it wrong. It's supposed to be this magnificent love story, right? A story of love lost and then found again. Yet, Rick gives the letters of transit to Victor, and Ilsa leaves *Casablanca* with him. It ruined the love story, if you ask me."

"What would you have had them do?"

"Rick should have kept the letters and left with Ilsa."

Michael nodded thoughtfully but not in agreement. "I can see that argument, but the funny thing is, John, the ending is one of the reasons I like it."

Morrison's interest now shifted from the movie to the gardener's character. "That's because you're an idealist, Michael Woofter. You and Atticus Finch and Andy Taylor even Oscar Grace. You're in good company," he teased.

Michael decided to himself it might be true. "Is that so bad? Being an idealist?" Michael queried.

"No, no Michael," Morrison assured him. "Just somewhat out of place."

Michael's questions and protests began to go astray, so Morrison deftly changed the subject to the recent power outage, leaving Michael to describe in detail what had happened.

"Kinda scary, isn't it?" Morrison said when Michael finished. "I've never known a failure like that aboard ship. We've had a few things in here fail, but nothing like that."

"Charles said the garden is more prone to an outage than anywhere else. Corrosion, he said, caused by all the water in the garden."

"What's corrosion?"

Michael realized Morrison's talents were strictly the arts not science. "Ah, well. Let's see. Oxygen and water can act on metal causing oxidation, which is known as corrosion. Did you ever notice in certain areas of the ship, in areas not normally accessible, an odd orange-red color tinting the metal works?"

Morrison nodded.

"Well, that's corrosion, and that's what happened to the circuit boxes," Michael said. By way of comparison, he looked around the media room. From eye level to the floor and continuing around three of the walls of the room were countless pieces of electronic equipment, pulsing and flashing lights, their display dials alive with activity. There were compact disk and DVD players, monitors, amplifiers, and still other gear designed to enhance or otherwise control the output of the other machines.

One large monitor displayed the film *Alien*, a perennial Mayflower favorite. Although the notion of sending people into outer space and later re-animating them was a source of intense amusement, the film was extremely popular. Possibly, because it was one of a mere few, the WSO had not edited in any way.

"You may not know what corrosion is, John, but I am amazed at your knowledge. You sure as hell know your movies and how to operate all this equipment."

Morrison laughed appreciatively. "I love movies, I guess, because it's in my blood. My ancestral parents were both professional actors before they joined the Project. And as far as the equipment goes, it's not as complicated as you might think. Maintenance is easy, too. The WSO packed along literally thousands of new units and parts, so repairs are fairly routine."

"But you also have to know how to make it all run," Michael marveled.

"True, but once you understand it, it's easy. Let's say I want to send a movie to ten different cabins. You simply channel the signal through this unit here," and Morrison pointed at a particularly complex-looking machine. "I can also send the same signal to every monitor aboard ship. I use this master unit when the Captain makes a ship-wide address. It can be locked to a pre-set volume, so that every monitor can only be controlled or turned off from here."

"That's one way to get your point across," Michael observed. "But I better go get some rest. So, you'll send along *Casablanca* then?"

"Sure, how about a double feature?" Morrison suggested.

"What do you have in mind?"

"Well, how many times have you seen *Alien*?"

"Hmmm. Good question. Maybe twenty times, I'd say."

"How do you feel about twenty-one?" Morrison asked humorously.

"Thanks, John, you're too kind."

"No, I'm not. I'm bribing you. You can leave some strawberries next to my cabin door."

# Chapter 30

After Michael left, Jamie settled in to her task of documenting the latest bounty. Meanwhile, working under Harmon's direction, the laborers deposited the plastic tubs brimming with fresh fruits and vegetables in the office. Jamie performed several analyses on random specimens of each type; weight, water, and sugar content were all tested and the results diligently recorded.

As work progressed, Jamie alerted the kitchen and a detail was dispatched to carry the food there for processing. The entire effort required nearly the whole shift, about five hours. Even so, after the harvest was completed and removed to the kitchen, Harmon remained and continued to work after the laborers left. Alone in the garden, he was putting the overripe food through a machine to separate pulp from seeds. Jamie glanced bemusedly through the window at him and smiled, marveling at his sense of dedication. The father was like the son in that respect. Michael also could work tirelessly at times, feeling as he did a profound responsibility for the food supply and the lives of his fellow travelers.

Jamie sat at the computer terminal, entering the data she compiled earlier. The office was still. The only sounds being the barely audible noises form the garden and the soft clicking her fingers made on the keyboard. On several occasions, her concentration was interrupted with an incipient thought. Something seemed…different. Something was subtly different.

She looked closely at her surroundings, taking a quick inventory of the room and its contents, but nothing was out of place. Nothing was missing. Shaking off these feelings of apprehension, she attributed them to the lingering fear triggered by the power failure. She refocused attention on her work and the softly glowing screen.

Wait! That was it! She realized in an instant. Where was the glare from the reflected light that was always present in the left corner of the screen? It was always there: a rectangular pattern of red and white dots reflected from the heavy locker door at the rear wall. She turned to look. The display was indeed out.

Very strange. She could not recall ever seeing those lights extinguished before. The power failure. That was it, she reasoned, but it also meant the time-lock was disengaged. In the WSO's infinite wisdom, they provided the Mayflower's children with an impregnable vault whose purpose was hidden from all but the very last generation. It was secured by a time-lock, which would reveal the secrets within only when the final destination was reached.

That was as much as anyone knew about it, including Michael or even Harmon. One does not question what one cannot hope to understand, so as a matter of practical necessity, this vault had never concerned Jamie previously. Obviously, the particular WSO engineer who designed this lock and its unique key never anticipated the simultaneous failure of the main power supply as well as the emergency systems.

Jamie weighed her options. Her first impulse was to let someone know what happened. Harmon? He was close at hand, but the garden was no longer his responsibility. Michael then, perhaps? No, he was probably asleep by now, so she thought better of it. It was, after all, hardly an emergency. She considered summoning the Perrys, but they were not on duty, and she was unsure what the procedural protocol would be. Should they look at the problem first? Or bring in others to correct their errors?

# Chapter 31

She finally decided to inspect it herself and make an evaluation before doing anything else. She approached the heavy door and placed a hand on the latch. With mild apprehension, she could hear and feel the internal mechanism respond to her touch as the lock disengaged. She pulled the massive door toward her and was more than a little surprised to find it deceptively weightless, despite its massive size.

Jamie peered nervously into the darkened chamber through the narrow slit, created by opening it slightly, but could see nothing. Guilty recriminations swept over her as she glanced toward the garden window, imagining for a moment Harmon may have witnessed this shameful scene. Relieved that he wasn't there after all, she considered closing the door, reversing any untold consequences she could have initiated by her transgression.

Taking a moment to clear her senses, she took inventory of what she had found so far. She almost laughed aloud at herself, realizing she had found out...nothing. With Michael absent, wasn't she the officer in charge? she reminded herself. If she failed to investigate this matter, and an unforeseen crisis resulted, couldn't she be held accountable for her lack of initiative?

The course of action was firmly decided. She now pulled the vault door wide, noticing an array of switches on the near wall, and struck each of them in turn. Only a few of the overhead lights responded, while some fluttered in a diminished glow and others remained dark. Another consequence of the power failure she reminded herself, reinforcing the decision to investigate the vault's secrets.

She stepped forward to begin exploring the room. Looking up, it had twenty-foot-high ceilings and was easily eighty feet deep. She estimated its floor space to be equal at least to the office but shaped into a narrow passageway. Had she stood with outstretched arms, it would have been possible for Jamie to touch each wall with her fingertips. As she took in her surroundings, she was struck by the fact that the last people to have entered here would have been the Mayflower's builders.

Installed along both walls from the floor to just slightly over her head were small file drawers which spanned the length of the vault. At the farthest wall were what appeared to be freezers. Stacked floor to ceiling, they were not unlike those found in the kitchen, except these were much larger.

What was this place, she asked herself? Her emotions wavered between amusement and disgust. All of this, the heavy steel door, the complicated time-lock, why had the architects of the Mayflower designed this room with these elaborate safeguards? All to protect some freezers and filing cabinets?

To satisfy her curiosities, she turned to examine the filing drawers, and the closest one at eye level drew her attention. She stepped close to read its inscription:

Apple (*Malus Sylvestris*)
planting – optimal site and climatic requirements

Below this drawer were others related to the same topic:

Apple (*Malus Sylvestris*)

– raising –

Apple (*Malus Sylvestris*)

– managing –

Apple (*Malus Sylvestris*)

– harvesting –

She knelt low to read more labels: apricot, araroba, beechnut; then stood tall, stretching to inspect those overhead. No surprise – while the names were largely unfamiliar, they all dealt with agricultural topics.

Jamie progressed further into the vault, scanning quickly the hundreds of files at random on both sides. Reaching the freezers, she stood in awe before them, knowing at once they were operable, feeling the intense cold radiating from the stainless-steel doors. Built into the bulkhead and stacked ten high and two wide, it was a misnomer to call them "freezers." Although the term would have been functionally appropriate, it was technically incorrect. It would have been more accurate to call them ovens, because cooling was accomplished passively by tapping into the cosmic chill, striking a balance with heat drawn from the Mayflower's reactors. The WSO engineers had turned the outer hull into a sophisticated heat exchange system, holding the cache of seeds at a constant $-120°C$. Ingeniously, the design insured there were no moving parts to wear out, requiring no maintenance intervention.

Jamie was satisfied everything was in order. As she approached the vault door, she would need to inform the Perrys that the system…the system…was secure." Why did they use a time-lock?" she said aloud rhetorically. It only made sense if there was something to keep hidden, she reasoned. If not the seeds, then why? It had to be something else. She looked back over her shoulder at the hundreds of file drawers. What was in those files?

Impulsively she opened the nearest drawer. It was the first one she looked at earlier:

> Apple (*Malus Sylvestris*)
> planting – optimal site and climatic requirements

It opened silently and smoothly, and inside lay an iridescent disk. Taking it out, she read the label and held it contemplatively as it reflected rainbows of light from its surface. This could be a magnificent opportunity, she realized; to look at once into her descendants' future as well as her ancestral past. This chance would not come again. Even so, the more she considered it, the more her curiosity turned to apprehension, forcing her to return the relic to its proper place. Reluctantly, she shut off the lights and carefully closed the vault door.

# Chapter 32

Jamie wondered again as she faced the empty office if her violation of the vault had been observed. Harmon could have easily looked through the garden window and noticed the door was open, but the sound of the elder gardener still hard at work dispelled her fears. She seated herself at the computer but had difficulty concentrating. Time and again, her thoughts strayed to the vault. Why not look? There would be no second chance once maintenance corrected the faulty time-lock, not in her lifetime. Anyway, who would know?

Jamie struggled with a new emotion, like the middle ground between defiance and surrender. How did the WSO have the right to suppress information across time and space only to grant special privilege to the last Mayflower generations? Why not look, she concluded, and decide for herself?

With firm resolve, she returned to the vault and removed the disk, then loaded it into the computer. She waited impatiently for the machine to respond, but just as the screen began its display, Harmon entered the air-lock. Jamie watched him over the top of the monitor as he peeled his raingear. She killed the play mode just as he came through the door.

"Got it all done," he announced briskly. "Michael should be happy about that, I hope. Everything is sorted and cleaned, and I put all the waste in the fertilizer bins so he can start on that his next shift."

Jamie's response was a blank look, and Harmon stopped to look closely at his daughter-in-law. Her face conveyed fear, but Harmon decided she was merely fatigued. "How's the filing going, then? You look like you could use some rest, for sure."

"It's actually going fine," Jamie proclaimed. "There's been a few distractions, though." Wait! She felt a sudden rush of panic and tried to look surreptitiously behind her. She had left the vault door slightly open. She became fixated on Harmon's eyes, following their movement, fearing he would notice. He didn't.

"You know, I have to say, you've been doing a great job here, Jamie, ever since you took over the number two spot. You just might be as good as Michael ever was," Harmon said, chuckling. "But don't tell him I said so. I only wish I could do as much as I used to, but these hands," he said ruefully, and rubbed each in turn. Jamie noticed how badly distorted his knuckles were. "Doctor said it's called 'arthritis,' but all I know is sometimes they hurt like hell."

"I'm sorry, Dad," Jamie said sympathetically.

"Oh, nothing to be sorry for," Harmon said dismissively. "Not your fault. But if you're finished, I'll walk you to your cabin."

"Well...no, that's okay. I'm really...I'm not done yet," Jamie lied. She also neglected to mention the time-lock, which was some form of lie – sin by omission. "I'll feel much better about it if I get it out of the way now rather than leave it for later."

"Dedicated, huh? That's the Woofter spirit," Harmon said, then yawned and stretched. "Ahh, boy. Well, fair enough, then. I'm off to bed, but I'll see you both later. I know you'll be meeting with Audrey Lester, so let me know about all that."

"Oh, yes, of course. We will, Dad, thank you."

After Harmon left, Jamie closed the vault door, but waited before turning her attention back to the enigmatic disk. She debated sharing this with Michael, or should she evaluate it first by herself. Harmon had praised her capabilities. Couldn't she judge the disk's significance as well as her husband? But there was also a chance Michael might strongly disapprove of what she had done so far.

The office door opened, casting light from the outer corridor on the wall beside her. *Michael?* Jamie thought. However, she was surprised to see it was Charles Perry and was relieved she waited before running the disk.

"Oh, Jamie. I didn't expect to find anyone here," Charles said cheerily. "I thought I could get in and out without anyone seeing me."

"Really, Charles? Why is that?" she asked nervously.

"No one likes to admit they didn't do their job, that's why. I just started my shift a while ago, and when I looked over the circuit map as I do every shift, I could see there was still something wrong in here."

"There is? I don't know, Charles. I haven't noticed. There doesn't seem to be anything wrong. Do you think you should check your circuit map again to be sure? But I'm really surprised you missed anything, you're so thorough."

"Well, thanks. I try. Anyway, when I went to the computer to trace it," he pointed at the vault. There it is. Now I can see the problem: the time-lock on the vault is out."

Jamie looked over in feigned amazement. "I…didn't…I should have seen that myself."

Charles walked over to the door. "See this empty pad? These lights are supposed to be on. It's understandable you wouldn't have seen it was out unless you were looking for it."

"I've noticed before those lights are usually lit. Is it going to be hard to fix?"

"No, it doesn't need repaired, just reprogrammed. All I have to do is this," and Charles began punching in a complex series of commands. "This is the reset sequence. It'll correct itself. Watch."

After flashing in random patterns, the light show suddenly stopped, leaving only certain ones lit.

"There you are. Safe and secure."

"Safe and secure," Jamie repeated blankly.

# Chapter 33

Michael did not return to his cabin after leaving the media center. Instead, he stopped at the cafeteria for a light meal, knowing the food would be straight from the harvest. Grabbing utensils and a tray, he stepped into the serving line.

"Everything looked really good this time, Michael," Mandy Friesen, head of kitchen operations said. "I swear, those tomatoes they brought in here were as big as asteroids."

Michael gave Mandy an overly serious expression. "No, I don't think so," he said slowly and deliberately. "I'd say they were more like comets."

"Oh, you're so smart," she scolded. "If you're so good, I'll just hand you some seeds, and you can start your own lunch from scratch."

"Well, I don't think that will work. I'm not as good a cook as you and besides, I'm a little hungry…"

"Yeah, I guess it's not right to deny the gardener his fair share. How does some of my famous tomato steaks sound? Mandy said, picking up a spatula in anticipation."

"It sounds like I'll take two," Michael smiled with enthusiasm and held out his tray to receive her offering.

"Michael, please join us." A voice invited from behind. It was Albert Breck, who was sitting with his wife, Patrice, at the nearest table. Albert was a lab technician while Patrice worked with John Friesen in the manufacturing section as a weaver/seamstress.

"Join us? Why?" Michael asked. "Are you coming apart?"

"You're primed, Michael," Albert laughed.

"I'll bet I know why, too. I understand Michael and Jamie have been talking with Audrey Lester," said Patrice knowingly. Michael admitted it was true. "But how did you know that?" he asked.

"We are, too," she replied with a lilt in her voice as she reached across the table for her husband's hand. "It's just common knowledge, Michael."

"That's wonderful," Patrice smiled happily at the gardener. "We've been told our ancestral analysis is complete, and Audrey advised us to 'get on the list,' as she said, because others will be confirming soon."

"We also went through the analysis, and I suppose she wants to talk to us about the results."

"I've been hearing you may get approved for natural conception."

"What else do you know, Patrice?" Michael asked, amazed at the extent of her information.

"Oh, I don't know. It's common knowledge, Michael," Patrice said, exasperated at having to repeat herself. "What's the difference? I think we'd be thrilled if Audrey approved us. But all the same, we'll just be happy to serve the Project."

While unspoken, the Mayflower community demanded sacrifices that always outweighed personal considerations. First of all, pregnancies had to be ordered and coordinated to avoid overwhelming the support systems and in accordance to the needs of the population. Genealogical records of the prospective couple had to be examined to ascertain if natural conception was permitted. If the family lineage ran too close, then sperm or egg taken from the frozen gene pool could be used to refresh the bloodlines.

"Remember, Michael, raising a child isn't like growing a pumpkin," a voice said. It was Captain Stratford, who had approached the table from behind the serving counter. He then sat down beside the gardener. "People can raise vegetables," he continued, and winked at Albert Breck. "But I'm not so sure a vegetable can raise a child."

Everyone laughed at Michael's expense, and the gardener pretended to be hurt. "A vegetable," he said plaintively. "Very cute, Captain." Michael then stood, making obvious his intention to leave. Placing his left hand on Captain Stratford's shoulder, he spoke conspiringly close to his ear.

"I only wish I had time to stay here for more verbal abuse, gentlemen, but I have more important things to do. Thank you all very much."

# Chapter 34

Michael felt his exhaustion when he returned to his cabin. Stretching out drowsily on the bed, he turned on the TV monitor. *John Morrison was as good as his word,* he thought. *Casablanca* was playing, as promised. Michael only watched it for a few minutes before falling into a deep sleep.

When he awakened the mantle of sleep persisted as he looked around, disoriented with his surroundings. The TV was still playing, only *Casablanca* had ended:

*Kane: Well, you should know; you know what it's made of.*
*Parker: No, man. I don't want to talk about what it's made of – I'm eating this.*
*Kane: (choking)*
*Parker: What's the matter? The food ain't that bad, baby.*
*Dallas: What? Kane, what's the matter?*

Michael swung his legs suddenly over the side of the bed as the scene played on. Damn it! He was supposed to make that appointment!

Shaking his head and reproaching himself, he reached for the phone and placed the call.

"Maternity, Audrey speaking."

"Audrey, it's Michael. Jamie told me you wanted us to set up an appointment."

"That's right," Audrey affirmed pleasantly. "When would be a good time for you both?"

"Actually, I would have called you earlier, but I just woke up," Michael's explanation amounted to an apology of sorts.

"Oh, it's okay. So, when would be a good time?"

"Well, I'm expecting her at the end of her shift, which should be pretty soon."

Michael checked the wall clock. "How about we come over as soon as she gets back, if that's alright?"

"That would be fine. I just started my shift, so I'll be here for a while. Come over as soon as you can, then."

"Okay." Michael nervously cleared his throat. "I was just wondering, too. I understand you have the results of our ancestral analysis, Jamie's and mine. Do you think...is there anything you can tell me about it?"

Audrey laughed, but remained impassive. "Yes, there's a lot I could tell you. But I won't. I'm sorry, Michael. You realize the whole purpose of having a meeting is so we can discuss it together. I'm sure you understand my position."

"Yes, of course I do." Michael said agreeably. "It's just...obviously, we're hoping for natural conception, so I was only wanting..."

"I know what you're hoping for," said Audrey, significantly. "And I can easily guess what it is you want. But just the same, I'm sorry."

"I understand. We'll discuss it later, then, as soon as Jamie returns."

"Very good, Michael. I'm looking forward to seeing you both, almost as much as you are. We'll see you shortly, Bye."

Michael hung up the phone. As he sat back again on the bed and became relaxed, he contemplated whether there was time enough for more sleep, feeling as though he'd had none at all. He tugged the top blanket closer and shut his eyes. In a few minutes, he began to feel... suspended... isolated...adrift.

What was that sound? He heard something, and it pulled him back from the twilight zone. Lying very still, he listened closely. Yes, there was a repetitive clicking coming from the living area. He rolled over and looking through the doorway, was surprised to see Jamie sitting in the large recliner. With her face in profile, he thought she might be sleeping. As he watched, she pushed off the floor with her foot, causing the chair to rock slightly back and forth.

"What are you doing?" he asked quizzically as he entered the room. "How long have you been here?"

Jamie was visibly startled as he approached. "Nothing."

"Nothing? What does that mean?" demanded Michael.

"I…I thought you were asleep, that's all. I didn't want to wake you."

"When did you get back?"

"A little while ago. Not long."

Michael's queries had only produced coquettish, evasive answers. He approached Jamie and sat down on the arm of her chair resignedly and changed the subject.

"I made that appointment with Audrey. I told her we'd be over as soon as we could."

"Okay. That's good, Michael," she said distantly, as if retrieving a long-discarded memory, then rested her head against his side.

Michael responded by pulling her in closer. While her demeanor was totally out of character, he attributed it to the demands placed upon her during the recent harvest. "Did everything go alright after I left?" he asked. "I hope it wasn't too much for you."

"Yes, it went fine," she said, then offered an abbreviated account of Charles Perry's return to reset the time-lock on the storage vault door, failing to mention her exploration of the room as well as her discoveries.

"How about that," Michael remarked. "I guess Charles Perry isn't nearly as infallible as he thinks he is." He pondered this new insight, then returned to the moment. "Well sweetie, if there's anything you want to do first…" he said significantly.

Jamie shook her head.

"No? Well, in that case, I think we better be going."

# Chapter 35

The hospital complex was designed like a half-wheel, with reception centrally located with each of the branches radiating outward from the hub. As they approached the reception area, Michael took Jamie's hand. "Are you nervous?" he whispered. "I know I am."

"Yes," she admitted quietly.

They both noticed upon entering that Captain Stratford and his young son David 217 were at that moment leaving reception for pediatrics. Having recently lost his wife, Laura, to cancer, the Woofters looked on sympathetically, knowing a heightened responsibility had befallen the Captain as a widower and single parent.

"Welcome, welcome," Audrey said brightly as she greeted the couple. Belinda Collins, the receptionist on duty, waved the Woofters through. "We'll have a lot to talk about, so let's go to my office." Audrey continued, turning on her heel to lead the way.

"Please," she said, indicating the seats before her work station once the door closed silently behind them. Looking at Michael and Jamie in turn, she opened the discussion. "I'm going to get quickly to the point. After all, we know why we're here. Isn't that right, Michael?" she said sternly, yet in a comical tone.

Michael's lips broke rank despite himself, displaying a wide, toothy grin. "First of all, on behalf of the Mayflower family, I have very happy news. Both of your ancestral analyses show you are cleared for natural conception." Audrey looked expectantly at the couple. Michael's smile expanded even wider, while Jamie continued to wear a strangely subdued and frozen expression.

"Congratulations," Audrey said warmly, yet failed to elicit any appreciable change in Jamie's demeanor, which stood in stark contrast with Michael's exuberance.

"Jamie," Audrey continued. "This will mean you'll have to undergo frequent exams, of course. I've scheduled your first one with Dr. Phen. In fact, he's waiting in the examination room right now if you'll..." Audrey had half risen from the chair, expecting Jamie to follow her. When she realized Jamie was disconnected from the conversation, unable to tear her gaze from her feet weighted heavily on the floor, Audrey sat down again.

Jamie finally managed to speak. "I realize all that. Thank you for everything, Audrey... I'd prefer...I'm just not prepared for anything like that right now."

Something assured Audrey this was not a negotiable point of contention, and she looked helplessly at Michael. "Is this something you both have talked about?"

Michael shook his head, almost imperceptively.

"Well, then I hardly know what to say, Jamie." She tapped out a few commands on her computer. "It would also be fine if we rescheduled later if you're concerned about it. But understand, too, we do have other couples who are anxious to begin their pregnancies, so this has to be carefully planned for and coordinated."

Jamie remained strangely unresponsive. *What could she be looking at?* Audrey thought to herself.

"Jamie," Michael spoke up sharply. "You need to do as Audrey has suggested. Dr. Phen is waiting, and I don't see any reason to delay..."

"I need some time," she said suddenly. Just as quickly, and with her face betraying some deep emotional conflict, she stood and left the room, the door closing silently behind her, leaving both Michael and Audrey in wonderment at her odd behavior.

"What was that?" Audrey spoke first in a bewildered tone. "I swear I've never...no one has ever acted like that. Do you have any idea what that was about?"

"I really don't know," he said helplessly. "But I want to apologize."

"Really, there's no need to, Michael" she assured him.

"Oh, I think there is. I want you to know she began acting strange after she finished up her last shift."

Audrey looked doubtful. "Do you think that would have anything to do with it? Maybe she's just nervous."

129

"No, I'm not trying to say there's a connection," Michael pointed out. "It's when it began, is all I'm saying. Perhaps, she's scared or nervous like you said, but I'll promise you one thing. I will get to the bottom of this, and I'll let you know what's going on."

"Fine, Michael," Audrey said, then stood up to indicate the meetings close. "Let me know as soon as possible so we can get Jamie re-scheduled."

# Chapter 36

Michael left and hurried back to the cabin. Predictably, he found Jamie sitting in the recliner as before.

"I'm sorry, Michael," she said as soon as he entered the room giving Michael a convenient opening.

"I was going to give you some time before I brought this up," he said, coming close and standing in front of her, but Jamie avoided his gaze. "But since you brought it up, tell me first that you're okay."

"I'm okay. I guess," she sighed heavily.

"Do you want to tell me what this is about?"

"I...I don't know. I'm not even sure I understand myself, Michael, what's happening to me."

"Jamie," Michael said gently and knelt down, taking both her hands in his. "There's no reason to be afraid. You have to know that. There is nothing you could tell me that would make me doubt you or love you any less than I do right now. Do you believe me?"

"Yes," she said, and looked into Michael's face, searching for his trust, as much as for his love.

"And you trust me?"

"You know I do," she said emphatically.

"Then tell me what this is about."

Jamie had to look away before she could begin. "I...didn't tell you...everything about what happened before." She admitted. "I'm sure you must have figured that out."

"Pretty much."

"The truth...the truth is, I already discovered the vault was unlocked before Charles returned. More than that...I went inside."

Michael grew contemplative, debating whether her violation constituted a breach of policy. Despite himself, however, his curiosity was piqued. "So, you looked inside. I guess there's nothing wrong with that, right? So, what was in there?"

Jamie described in detail the contents of the vault: the freezers containing seeds intended for the last Mayflower generation and the instructional disks held in the file drawers. While Michael listened patiently to her confession, he failed to make a connection between this discovery and her odd behavior in the maternity clinic. "And this is why you've been acting strange – because of the room?"

"Michael, no. It's not the room. It's—"

"What then?" he said impatiently.

Jamie gave pause, knowing her next admission hardly qualified as Mayflower policy, even if the inspection of the vault did. "I took a disk from its file," she said, dropping her head in shame. "Then Charles Perry showed up and reset the lock. But even though I hadn't watched it, I intended to put it back, but then I couldn't."

"You watched it after he left?"

"Yes."

"Where is it now?"

"I brought it back here," she pointed at the top drawer next to the computer.

Michael rose, and went to retrieve the mysterious relic, and slipped it into the computer.

"Michael, do you think…"

"I really don't know what to think. Whatever you saw that did this, I need to understand for myself."

"That's just it, Michael," Jamie pleaded. "Don't you see what it did to me? I don't want it to happen to you. Please don't look at it. Let's take it to the funerary room and flush it into space." She then fell silent, knowing there was no dissuading her husband, so she watched passively as the monitor displayed the encoded contents of the disk.

Michael was entranced at once, drawn into a vivid display of novel shapes and dimensions, unaware that as he watched, a part of him became irrevocably changed "Ain't this a bitch," he intoned quietly.

Truth is freedom.

Freedom is change.

Change is empowerment.

# Chapter 37

The phone beside the bed rang, awakening Captain Stratford. He continued lying motionless in the half-darkness, however, wrapping the crook of his arm across his eyes and allowed the answering machine to take the call.

"Captain, Audrey Lester here," the maternity clinic director's plaintive voice declared.

*Sounds a little urgent,* Stratford thought.

"I'm calling to apprise you of a recent situation that…I don't know…It looks like it'll require your input because I have no idea what else I can do. Please call me as soon as you get…"

Stratford quickly grabbed the receiver. "Audrey, yes, it's me."

"Oh, Captain, I'm sorry. Did I wake you?"

"Yes, actually you did," he admitted with a laugh. "But that's okay. It's just that after a while, you learn what's to be taken seriously and what can wait. I thought I'd better…talk to you right now, you sounded…well, anyhow, what do you need from me?"

"This may seem at first to be outside your expertise, so hear me out," Audrey began tentatively. "As you must know, we have to plan all pregnancies very carefully aboard this ship for obvious reasons."

"I'm aware of that."

"During the initial stage, we do an ancestral analysis of the candidates and then progress into other phases based on those results. In the case of the Woofters, we scheduled them to discuss all of that. It was during our meeting that Jamie refused an examination with Dr. Phen and left in an agitated state…and without, Michael, I might add."

"She did? That is strange." Stratford agreed. "Maybe she's just scared…have you talked to her about it?"

"No, I haven't. That's why I wanted your help."

"Okay, but I'm not sure what I can say that will make a difference. Frankly, I think you should speak to her first," Stratford suggested.

"I agree, and I've tried," Audrey said helplessly, her voice rising. "I haven't seen her or spoken to her since then. I don't think you quite understand, Captain. It's not for lack of trying. I've called many times and left messages. I've even gone to their cabin, but they have the entry grid off."

"What about Michael?"

"Oh, yes, I've seen him, and he promises to call or bring her to the clinic, but then...nothing."

"How long has this been going on?"

"I'm not sure. It seems like twenty, maybe thirty shifts, I guess."

"Is it possible she's sick?"

Audrey considered this for a moment. "Perhaps, but if she is, she hasn't been to the hospital. More to the point, though, I understand Michael has been bringing all her meals to their cabin. She hasn't been seen, and she hasn't worked any of her shifts. Apparently, Harmon has taken them over."

Another line of thought occurred to Stratford. "What was the result of their ancestral analysis?" he asked suddenly.

"They both have clean blood lines, so I approved them for natural conception. Why?"

"I don't know. No reason," he said as if distracted. "It's just that...usually, it's taken as a point of honor, isn't it? Instead, they're acting like..."

Audrey knew what Stratford was trying to say, even if he didn't. "It's as if...they've renounced...us...or the Mayflower Project."

"It might seem like it." Stratford reluctantly agreed. "I know Woofter; he knows better. Something else must be wrong. I promise I'll make a point of seeing Michael during my rounds, and I'll let you know what I find out."

"Thank you, thank you...you have no idea what a relief that is." Audrey exhaled deeply. "We have to get them committed to a schedule; there are other couples we're trying to work with. Thank you again, Captain."

# Chapter 38

*First things first*, he thought to himself after he hung up. Sloughing off the last remnants of sleep, he climbed wearily from bed.

To Stratford's surprise, his son David Stratford 217 was standing fully dressed in the doorway to the bedroom. "Hello there, little skipper," he said brightly. "You're up early. You must have some big plans."

"Did you forget, Dad?" the boy chided his father. "My class gets to see the 'lympia, so I already been up a long time."

"It's Oh-lympia."

"I know. Olympia."

"No, David, I didn't forget. How could I?" Stratford protested playfully. "It's the only thing you've talked about lately."

As part of their ongoing education, all children were instructed in the history and operation of the Mayflower from bow to stern. Yet, it was the Olympia that held the greatest fascination, being the inexorable link between the Mayflower's departure and that future finite moment of its abandonment and the completion of the Project.

David sat down on the bed next to his father. "You can fly the Olympia, can't you?"

"If I had to, yes. I suppose I could. Why?"

"Because I told Eddie da Silva you could, but he said it can't be flown 'til the Mayflower gets to Tau Ceti," David said heatedly.

"Well, skipper, there's no reason to get upset," Stratford said as he wrapped his hand across David's shoulder. "Eddie's partly right. It's not that the Olympia can't be flown. It won't be flown. Since the Mayflower is incapable of landing, the Olympia will be used once Earth 2.0 is approached so the last generation can disembark…uh, leave the Mayflower."

"Why can't it land?"

"Because it's too big, and it wasn't designed to land."

Observing the crestfallen look on David's face, Stratford continued on an upbeat note. "Just the same, David, I could fly the Olympia. It's part of being Captain, part of the training. Someday, it will be up to you to pass that knowledge on to your son, probably."

He then pulled David close. "Thanks for defending my honor," he teased. "No more questions now, please. Let me get ready so we can have our breakfast, and then, you can go learn all you want about the Olympia."

"Okay," David said quietly. "But when we studied about the Mayflower Project, Mrs. da Silva said only the best people were allowed to come, 'cause they had to save our kind. We're important, aren't we? We're helping, too…right, Dad?"

"Yes, of course that's right." Stratford affirmed. "But enough already. Shove off, young skipper." He lifted David off the bed.

As the Mayflower ever distanced itself from Earth through space and time, so proportionally had the Project's legend swelled, and so grew the mythology of its scope and purpose. The first generation was taken as heroes, privileged participants, or even saviors. They were seen as those propagating their species and saving them from a doomed planet, while all other generations were the congregation, so to speak.

As father and son approached the cafeteria, David suddenly broke stride to run ahead. His closest friend, Eddie da Silva had arrived, accompanied by his parents, Ramon and Katherine. Eddie also began to run once he noticed David.

The boys were joined by their other classmates who were also anticipating touring the Olympia, including Rachel Collins, David's special sweetheart. Stratford was amused as he watched Rachel petulantly insert herself into the midst of the children and extract David by the hand, leading him away to the serving line.

*He needs to be more assertive,* he thought to himself.

"The kids all seem pretty excited about the Olympia," a low voice said from behind. It was Charles Perry.

"Yes. If David is any indicator, I'd agree with you, Charles," Stratford confirmed. "He's been looking forward to it, I can tell you."

Both men watched now as David stood up suddenly, demonstrating to his companions some difficult maneuver of an invisible space shuttle. He had his arms outstretched and pretended to manipulate the controls.

"David...take a look at Woofter," Perry said, indicating the direction with a slight jab of his elbow.

Indeed, the gardener was a curious sight. He had entered the cafeteria with his head bowed low, avoiding contact with everyone. As they continued to watch in fascination, he proceeded directly to the serving line.

"You know, I haven't seen him around in quite a while," Perry declared. "Jamie either, for that matter. I've heard Harmon has taken over her work schedule."

Stratford withheld comment but nodded in agreement.

"Did you notice?" Perry whispered excitedly. "He's taking two of everything they have; he must have come for both of them."

Michael quickly left the line with his heaping tray of food, but instead of taking a seat, he turned and scurried toward the entrance, confirming Perry's assertion he was foraging for himself and Jamie.

As he began to leave, he glanced nervously over his shoulder and looked in the direction of Stratford and Perry. He appeared visibly upset, possibly because his actions had been observed. Yet, there was an air of defiance about him, too. Then, in a moment, he was gone.

"He looked right at us," Perry said.

"Through us, I'd say," Stratford added wryly. In truth, though, Stratford thought Michael had been looking only at him.

"Oh, well, it's hard to tell what's up with him. I guess I'd better round up the kids for the big event," Perry declared, breaking into Stratford's reverie. "Why don't you come along? After all, you're probably more qualified than me to discuss the Olympia."

Stratford smiled slightly. "I'd like to, Charles, but I have some things I have to attend to."

"Some things?" Perry asked inquiringly.

Stratford had already started walking away, but turned and nodded to Perry.

"Yeah, Woofter, for one," he said.

137

# Chapter 39

"Hello, Captain," Ramon da Silva looked up from the massive console in front of him when Stratford entered the control room. He seldom visited there. He didn't need to. The ship's guidance computers operated in a seamless cybergenic union conceived by man and enabled by machine. At most, the navigational program required occasional minute adjustments to correct the Mayflower's drift in direction and speed. Ramon was doing just that: "tweaking the wobble," as it was called.

"Hard at work, I see," Stratford responded to Ramon's greeting.

Ramon grinned broadly. "No, not really. It's just a matter of feeding the system the information." He tapped on the keyboard a few times to illustrate.

Stratford had only partly listened to Ramon's answer. He became immediately drawn to the view of the darkened starscape at the Mayflower's leading edge. He stood in the center of the observational canopy, awestruck. This wedge of pure crystal was cut from a solid slab, polished and perfect, giving an unobstructed view of all forward directions at once. The visual effect was as if one's own essence was being hurled unencumbered through space.

"That's some view, huh?"

Stratford receded at Ramon's comment, back to a less ethereal place.

"It doesn't change much, though," Ramon added.

Stratford agreed. It had never changed in his memory or lifetime for that matter. Perhaps, there was something comforting about that.

An assortment of indicator lights began flashing across the console in a random procession. "I'm almost finished here," Ramon said as a statement of fact more than for Stratford's edification. He locked in the new coordinates, prompting the computer to respond as an obedient student might obey its master.

Stratford came closer and watched in deep admiration of the pupil as much as for the teacher. "What would happen if we failed to correct for drift?" he asked.

"Not as much as you might think," Ramon responded. "A minute of arc, translated over, say, a hundred years would certainly put us off course, but given the size of the target, we could also manually correct for it and still not miss it."

He pointed at the observational canopy. "Look out there. Notice that group of three: Tau Ceti is already the brightest star among them. Do you see it?"

"Yes. I know where it is." Stratford answered assuredly.

"Then how could you miss it?"

Stratford was about to concede Ramon's point when a momentary flash of light from behind attracted both men's attention, the source being from the well-lit outer concourse. The door had opened, admitting the light, and to Stratford's considerable surprise, Michael Woofter stood in the entrance.

Strangely, he stood perfectly motionless, his body rotated slightly as if contemplating making an exit.

"Excuse me," he apologized softly. His eyes appeared unfocused as he blankly looked anywhere. Specifically, he looked everywhere except at Ramon or Stratford. "I didn't expect...I wanted to talk to you, Captain."

Ramon threw an inquiring look at Stratford, who maintained his gaze upon the gardener. "I'm finished here, I was just telling the Captain," Ramon announced, offering his excuse to leave. He rightly assumed that whatever Michael planned to discuss with Captain Stratford, he didn't want to share with him or anyone else.

# Chapter 40

Once Ramon left, Stratford sat in his vacated seat and gestured for Michael to take the adjoining one. The gardener came close, hesitantly, but declined to sit.

"I knew you'd be looking for me," Michael said, explaining his presence.

"That's true," Stratford confirmed. "I was planning on leaving here and going directly to the garden. I assume you have an idea what I wanted to see you about."

Michael looked boldly at Stratford, almost defiantly. "Yes, I know why."

"Then you must know Audrey asked me to speak to you."

Michael shrugged and nodded slightly.

"I understand Jamie hasn't followed through with her required exam, and of course, Audrey is concerned. You realize there are other couples whose pregnancies must be planned for," Stratford paused, allowing Michael a chance to respond.

The gardener remained strangely silent.

"Look, Michael, I also have to know Jamie's all right," Stratford said, suppressing his growing impatience. "I've heard she's not working any of her shifts and that Harmon has taken them over."

"Don't worry, Captain. She's actually…she's fine."

"In that case, let's get her scheduled with maternity," Stratford said briskly, reaching for the phone. Michael intercepted his move by quickly placing a hand over the receiver.

"Wait, Captain. I should tell you this. We've decided, Jamie and I, not to proceed."

The gardener's words rang hollow as Stratford strained to grasp his meaning. "What do you mean 'not proceed'? What the hell are you saying? Is Jamie already pregnant?"

"No, she's not. What I'm saying is we've decided not to conceive."

Stratford was stunned by his admission. Yet, he sensed Michael was leading to this from the outset.

"Here's why that's not an option," he lectured as if to a child. "The Project's purpose is to transport our kind to a new world. We wouldn't even be here if it wasn't for that. We have to reproduce, Michael, or the Project fails."

"Yes, but it's not our purpose, Captain. Not anymore," Michael countered.

Stratford forced himself to look away. He gazed out the observational canopy, seeking composure and reconnected with the view of Tau Ceti. He turned to face the gardener; his confidence restored. "What's happened to you…both of you? Do you somehow think you're the only ones aboard this ship? We're all dependent on each other, Michael, and a decision like that is not yours alone to make. The completion of the Project depends upon our mutual cooperation."

"We understand all that."

"Well, then, what is it? If it's a matter of counseling, I know Audrey and Dr. Phen would do anything to help Jamie through her…problems."

"Counseling?" the gardener asked sarcastically. "Do you really think so? That should fix everything nicely."

Michael had once revered his Mayflower birthright, holding as Stratford did an unwavering belief in the Project's higher purpose. He also realized that man's deepest convictions can't be bargained for or negotiated. Something important stood to be gained here by trying. He laughed quietly, standing before the Captain with his head bowed low by the weight of the moral irony separating his and Stratford's disparate ideals. Despite the consequences, he knew he had to try.

"Tell me there's an explanation for all of this," Stratford demanded.

"There is," the gardener said and extracted a plastic disk from inside his uniform. He held it contemplatively as it reflected rainbows of light, forcing Stratford to turn away.

"What's that?"

"In a manner of speaking, the truth, but it's better I show you rather than try to explain it," he said, then loaded the computer.

Instantly, the large overhead monitor displayed titles and production credits leaving Stratford to absorb only scant details as he watched. "Where did you get this?" he asked, awestruck, then realized: this had been produced by the WSO.

Michael explained briefly how the garden's power failure had left the time-lock on the storage vault disengaged, leaving Jamie to accidentally make the discovery.

Stratford did not yet understand the connection. "This video you are showing me…this explains everything?" he asked incredulously.

Michael nodded. "Just watch."

The screen filled with novel images, dimensions, and even colors unknown to Stratford's experience. The predominant color was pale blue, a hue much lighter even than Michael Woofter's eyes. It filled the entire background that was beginning to unfold.

A transport vehicle wheeled slowly over a well-rutted lane, stopping at the edge of a vast cultivated area. Seemingly countless rows of young trees stretched from the foreground into a far horizon of green. Stratford watched as two workmen stepped from the truck and lifted bundled saplings from the back and placed them in shallow holes. They heaped dark brown soil around each plant in turn with shovels.

The visual perspective disoriented Stratford at first, being familiar only with the impenetrable view of deep space or distances found in the confines of the Mayflower. He briefly considered this was leftover footage from some Hollywood production, and whatever parallels the Woofters had drawn about its significance to the Mayflower Project had to be erroneous. He could think of no name to call this place or the plants that grew therein. It was a nascent orchard.

In a strange counterpoint to Stratford's internal monologue, an unseen narrator began to speak. It was a male voice, pleasant sounding and nondescript. While the words he spoke were benign, in the context of deep space seemed altogether inane and other worldly:

"…While the conditions encountered on Earth 2.0 might vary greatly from those of Earth, the seeds of *Malus Sylvestris* will result in many different varieties. Through hybridizing, you will produce specimens of superior quality…"

The camera's eye then swept over and beyond the orchard, displaying jagged white-topped mountains rising in the distance. Cottony clouds curled over the peaks while the scene reflected in a glassy lake lying at their base.

Beyond all other wonders, he became transfixed by the pulsing circle of yellow-orange hung motionless behind the clouds. It was the source of light for this landscape as well as the source of life. Stratford knew instinctively: this was the Earth's star. It was the sun.

He looked aside from the magnificent spectacle to assess Michael's reaction.

"That's right, Captain," the gardener said, presumptive of Stratford's thoughts. "It's the Earth."

There was no question. This was the ancient Earth, or more precisely, 16,000-year-old digital pixels, produced as a gardening manual for the last Mayflower inhabitants. It had been under Dr. Keith Hardin's directive that the WSO expunged all visual records of Earth from the Mayflower's library of films, and Stratford realized how damning this visual document was. It contradicted the ancient myth that Earth had become overpopulated, contaminated, spent. This notion supposedly prompted the Mayflower Project. Their ancestors were the honored elite, chosen as the saviors of the human species. Dr. Hardin's directive insured the required blind devotion to the Project by preemptively crushing any rebellion before it could occur. He had theorized that in the absence of an alternate point of view, the Mayflower's children would embrace the only world they knew.

Michael switched off the system, and the overhead monitor went black. Then, he extracted the disk and returned it to his uniform. He glanced at Stratford, who appeared subdued, slumped back in his chair. "Are you alright?" he asked the Captain solicitously.

Stratford exhaled deeply, rubbing the back of his hand across his face. He had not yet assimilated the deeper significance of what he had just seen, but he understood it's power. "Yes, I'm alright," he said, preoccupied with other thoughts. "Has anyone else seen this?"

"No, just Jamie and I."

"Not even your father?"

"No, sir," the gardener avowed, neglecting to mention Harmon's refusal to look at the disk when Michael told him about it. "Not yet."

"Well...that's good, then. We're going to keep it that way, too. Let's have it," Stratford demanded extending his open hand expectantly.

Michael understood Stratford's intent: to suppress. He reached toward the disk hesitantly, placing his palm across the outside of his uniform in an act of both compliance and defiance but said nothing.

Stratford chose to ignore this display of rebellion for the moment. "No one was supposed to see that until the completion of the Project," he reminded Michael.

"I didn't show it to you for your entertainment," said Michael sarcastically. "You wanted to know why Jamie and I rejected procreation. Right? Well, it's all there, Captain," he said, tapping his chest significantly. "You saw it all."

"Yes, I did, and I've also seen what it's done to you," Stratford retorted.

This last comment struck hard, and Michael grew quietly reflective. "I have to tell you." No one ever believed in the Mayflower Project more than I did – no one. I always thought we were here to preserve humanity…but I understand now. We're part of this because…no, let me rephrase that. Our DNA is part of this because our ancestors volunteered, but we had no say in it, Captain. Not me, not Jamie, not you, and certainly not our children.

Stratford started to interject, but Michael cut him off. "Please, just hear me out. I'd thought, as we all did, that the scenes of Earth were missing from the films to shelter us from images of the dying Earth, but it's a lie. It was to prevent us from seeing the world that was taken from us. So, it's very simple, Captain. We're respectfully declining any further participation in the Mayflower Project, and with your permission, we want to share this discovery with the rest…"

"Request denied," Stratford snapped. He had listened to the gardener's arguments but was reminded that Michael failed to appreciate the larger point of view. This Project was the greatest of all scientific endeavors and would fade to insignificance if not completed. He also thought about his ancestral father's personal glory, as well as his own inherited birthright as the 216th Captain of the Mayflower expedition. "How exactly do you 'decline,'" Stratford continued, his voice edged with emotion.

"By not committing another innocent life to the Mayflower Project."

"Where do you think we are, Michael," Stratford exploded in rage. "There's no 'declining' on a space craft – it's a one-way commitment, and we're all dependent upon each other."

"They'll decide that for themselves once they learn the truth. Then the Project dies of attrition."

"You will not make the sacrifices of my ancestors meaningless," Stratford shouted, slamming his fist into the armrest as he swung the chair around to face the gardener. The suddenness of Stratford's anger took Michael aback. "The Project will be completed," Stratford vowed.

"The Project be damned. Our lives have meaning, too, Captain – quite apart from your ancestors or even mine," Michael argued. "And after we've shown this to the crew, I believe…"

"Again, permission denied. In fact, I order you to turn that disk over to me, and you are to forget about its contents. I forbid you to discuss it with anyone. Is that understood?"

Michael had already turned to leave, seemingly oblivious to Stratford.

"You have no right to supersede my authority," Stratford warned. "And you can't force your will on the members of this ship, Michael. We're dropping this, right?"

Glancing over his shoulder for the briefest of moments, the gardener's silence was in defiance of Stratford's order, disguised though it was as a request. Approaching the control room door, it opened and closed noiselessly as Michael passed through to the concourse beyond, leaving Stratford alone.

# Chapter 41

Audrey Lester had listened attentively to Captain Stratford, sitting face to face with him in her office. "To tell you the truth, Audrey, I'm not convinced it made any difference," Stratford confessed as he described the conversation they had earlier.

"Did he ever make clear what it is that's troubling Jamie?" she asked.

Leaving out the details of Jamie's discovery, he emphasized that their decision to forego childbearing appeared to be mutual.

Audrey held out both arms, palms upturned in a gesture acknowledging Stratford's authority. "Well, Captain, I'm sure you realize something has to be done, but it's up to you to make the final call."

Stratford's response was a tacit agreement. "What kind of choices do we have here?"

"There's really only one, artificial insemination."

"Do you believe it's the only…it has to go that far?"

"Yes, I do. I know it's outside your area. Let me take care of it. All I need is your approval and permission to proceed."

"You have it then," he said doubtfully. "You're sure about this?"

"Captain, let me ask you: do you know anything about raising food," Audrey asked pointedly.

"No," Stratford admitted. "Why?"

"Neither do I."

# Chapter 42

Jamie struggled against the mental fog that weighted her consciousness and distorted her senses. Upon reawakening, she heard a series of low indiscernible human voices but was unable to identify any of them. They moved randomly about this room in which she found herself, but inexplicably, she could not open her eyes and had no idea how many there were. She focused her concentration and attempted to count them: "One…two…there's two…" she recited with thickened tongue, becoming thoroughly confused with her task and so stopped trying.

"Why is she doing that?" Jamie heard a disembodied voice. Was it Captain Stratford? say, but it went apparently unanswered.

Suddenly, someone placed a hand upon her brow; gently, strands of her dampened hair were being brushed aside. She tried vainly to react, commanding the nerve pathways but had no use of her hands and could not move her legs.

Her eyelids were pulled back in turn, and someone flashed a small beam of light briefly into each pupil. "Jamie?" another voice spoke louder than the first. This was Dr. Phen. "Can you hear me?" Although she moaned faintly and turned her head away, it was in avoidance of the painful light.

With eyes swimming and perceptions askew, she saw an expanse of yellow-orange extending from the edge of her visual field. It was the paper she was laying on, made from the husks of squash raised in the garden. However, here she was naked on an examination table in this small room in the maternity center.

"I believe she's ready now," Dr. Phen pronounced after his examination.

As she listened to his voice, his words the previous events were brought into focus as Jamie recalled what happened. It was after Michael left for the garden. They had entered her cabin, uninvited; that is, Dr. Phen, Audrey, Martin Collins, and Captain Stratford. Opening the door manually, they restrained her while Audrey delivered a stabbing pain to her arm, and she awoke in here. Even in her fragile and weakened emotional state, she knew why. She'd been expecting this.

"Audrey, reposition the thin man fully extended," Dr. Phen requested as the maternity director turned away to comply. Immediately, Jamie felt her limbs being pulled independent of her will, arms taut above her head, legs spread. The "thin man," as it was euphemistically called, was the device attached to the overhead that was used for artificial insemination. It both restrained and supported the subject, having the unsettling appearance of a stick figure of grotesque proportions. This "thin man" consisted of an elongated neck and head for illumination, as well as two sets of arms and legs with restraint cuffs to grasp the wrists and ankles. At the thin man's waist was the phallic – like delivery tube in which a charge of donor seed was placed.

"I'll have to first remove her pessary implant," the doctor continued, then began to wash his hands. "Audrey, if you will please initiate first stage reanimation and program our skinny friend to run the entire sequence, I think we can begin."

Audrey first loaded the insertion tube with a vial of sperm, human essence from an ancient donor long dead and long forgotten. It was this triumph of man's genome over time and space that rendered all other human endeavors inconsequential. Including, in a perfect paradox, the Mayflower Project.

Stratford watched the thin man move convulsively to Audrey's command as Jamie mirrored his every move in a horrific choreography. He became repulsed by the display. "Doctor, if you'll excuse me, I think I'll step outside for the rest of this if you don't mind," he said uneasily.

"No, of course not, Captain. There should be no complications, but if you would remain outside till we're through, in case Michael…you understand. We may require your…influence." Dr. Phen said, then addressed Martin Collins. "You may step out too, if you wish, Martin, but perhaps you could remain with Captain Stratford…" His voice trailed off, leaving the obvious implications unspoken.

# Chapter 43

Stratford and Martin left the doctor and Audrey to their task, proceeding through a short, dimly-lit maze to the hospital's reception area.

"Looks like it's full up," Stratford said as he looked for two adjoining seats. Finding none, he led Martin to stand near the main entrance door.

"I'm glad you said something back there, Captain," Martin said gratefully in a low voice. "I'd already seen more than I wanted, I can tell you."

Stratford managed to give a tight-lipped smile that neither confirmed or denied.

"Frankly, I'm not sure what that was about," Martin continued. "I mean…what's wrong with Jamie, anyhow, that they had to bring her in like that? I've only heard rumors, but she hasn't been in the garden for I don't know how long. All Dr. Phen would tell me was to meet him at the Woofter's cabin. He didn't say why, or that we'd be…we'd be doing something like *this*. I don't know; it doesn't seem right."

"Maybe not," Stratford agreed but didn't attempt to elaborate. He became preoccupied with the rumors Martin alluded to. He was certain the Woofters hadn't shared Jamie's discovery with anyone else. He would have heard all about it. After questioning Michael, he managed to avoid making a full disclosure to Audrey and Dr. Phen, the most powerful lie being a half-truth, so they only thought it was an emotional crisis over child-bearing that had caused Jamie's emotional breakdown. As distasteful as forced impregnation seemed even to Stratford, he believed a greater good was being served, and he felt justified to leave it at that. Afterward, the Woofters would again embrace the Mayflower Project with the same dedication they had before becoming… tainted.

"I'm sure she had her reasons, no matter how misguided they were," Stratford responded evasively to Martin's comments. "But after she has a child to raise, I'm sure they'll put aside this nonsense…"

"Say, look who's coming," Martin interrupted excitedly.

Stratford had noticed his approach, too. Looking through the door's heavy glass portal, they saw the gardener approaching on the main corridor, his stride hurried and purposeful. Noticing Stratford and Martin, his destination became obvious when he quickened his pace.

Both men prepared themselves reflexively when Woofter stepped into the room.

"Jamie's in there?" he said, being both question and statement of fact. While he didn't look directly at either man, he intended his remark for Stratford. "I want to see her."

Martin stood to Woofter's right. Looking down, he noticed him flexing his hand into a tight fist and prepared to react if necessary.

"That isn't possible just yet, Michael," Stratford said soothingly.

"I intend to see her, Captain."

While Martin alone would have been deterrent enough because of his size, Woofter also respected Stratford's authority. Taking in the reception area, he saw there were more than a few men scattered amongst several women. Sensibly, he knew he would not prevail.

Stratford rested a hand on Michael's shoulder in a show of sympathy, yet Michael interpreted the gesture as one of restraint. "Don't worry, you will. But you have to understand – Jamie is…she's under Dr. Phen's care, so it's his call."

"Then announce me to Dr. Phen."

Stratford looked hard at Michael and was taken aback at this confidence he was displaying. It bordered on aggression.

"I'll take care of it, Captain," Martin volunteered, and walked over to the receptionist. After a brief discussion, she placed a call and relayed the response to Martin. He turned, nodding affirmatively.

"Looks like it's okay. But before we go back there, I want to remind you where you are and that you're both still part of the Mayflower Project. What was done here had to be done."

"Save it, Captain," Michael answered icily. "There won't be any trouble."

Martin fell in behind the others as they went past the reception work station and traced their steps back to where they left Jamie. The doctor was waiting to escort them to her room, but he also wanted to observe Woofter's demeanor.

Could he be trusted? The relaxed manner Stratford displayed in the gardener's company was reassurance enough.

"Please, Captain…I would suggest we allow Michael time alone with Jamie," Dr. Phen pleasantly suggested, then addressed the gardener. "Understand though, Michael, Jamie has been sedated, and she will fall asleep quickly. So, please don't be too long. We will be in my office if you need us for any reason."

Michael regarded Dr. Phen and the others with a great deal of suspicion and so he waited until they left before entering Jamie's room. She was lying very still, loosely covered in a light blanket and apparently asleep. "Jamie?" he said softly.

She opened her eyes slowly, then wider. With a rush of emotion, she realized it was Michael.

"Oh, I'm so glad," she cried. "They came into our cabin and brought me here."

Michael imagined Jamie's abduction, adding anger to the sadness he had endured since learning the truth about the Mayflower Project. Sitting heavily on the bed, he reached for Jamie's hand. "I knew exactly what happened…when you weren't in the cabin. I knew."

"I'm so sorry, Michael."

"Sorry? You've nothing to be sorry for. Stratford and Phen may find they have more to be sorry for than you."

Jamie pulled herself closer to her husband. "Michael, there's nothing we can do. I don't want to fight them. Dr. Phen said this procedure is always successful. I'm going to have a baby. We cannot refuse the Project now. We will soon have a child to raise. We have no choice."

"There are always choices," Michael declared ominously.

"I don't want to fight this any longer. I'm only sorry I opened that vault, and what it's done to you. I'm sorry for everything." Jamie laid her head against Michael's arm as she slipped into unconsciousness. "We have to accept…accept what's happened…promise me," she said imploringly.

Michael nodded, but he had crossed over to an indeterminable place. When sadness and anger become fused, it turns to hatred.

# Chapter 44

Chuck Perry left the port side of the Mayflower in his ongoing search for Captain Stratford. He had already covered the starboard pretty thoroughly, as well as the cafeteria and engine room. Stratford's habit of taking in most areas of the ship on his normal rounds meant he could be anywhere. He had just been to Stratford's cabin and found it empty.

"Finally," he said to himself with much relief. Stratford was in view some distance ahead walking the main corridor accompanied by Ramon daSilva.

He broke into an easy jog. "Captain," he called out, prompting other Mayfloridians in his path to step hurriedly aside. "Hello there, Captain," he shouted again. This time, Stratford heard his name and both men stopped to wait for the younger Perry.

"Thank you, sir," Chuck said gratefully and bent slightly at the waist for a few quick sips of air. "I've looked all over for you. My dad said for me to bring you to the landing area."

*The landing area?* Stratford thought to himself. It was an odd request. He looked aside at Ramon. "Why? Are we expecting visitors?" he said and laughed, while Ramon joined in at Chuck's expense.

The younger Perry nodded good-naturedly and waited for the laughter to run its course.

"Did he say why?" Stratford asked at length.

"Yeah, he did, but I better let him discuss it with you," Chuck replied evasively, looking first at Ramon and then directly at the Captain, catching his eye.

Stratford understood at once the subtlety of what he was trying to convey, so did Ramon. "Well, if that's the case, Ramon, I'll have to catch up with you later," Stratford said briskly. Then, he turned to follow Chuck, leaving Ramon to proceed alone to the cafeteria.

A short walk brought them to the elevator connecting the main corridor to the upper level. Waiting there to take the lift as well, they encountered Second Officer Steve Lester and John Friesen, head of manufacturing. "Why, it's our illustrious Captain and the young electrician," Steve announced grandly. *Almost sarcastically*, Stratford thought, even as he held the door for the newcomers. "I guess we're sharing our ride, John."

Once the elevator began its slow ascent, Steve spoke up again. "What's the agenda, Captain?" he pointedly asked.

"We're going to the landing area," Chuck volunteered on Stratford's behalf, knowing full well the question was intended for the Captain.

"Great. That's even better. We were going to John's sector, but maybe we'll tag along with you instead. We've nowhere to be in particular, right John? And no one to see once we get there," Steve declared, patting Chuck's shoulder in a gesture of camaraderie. The effect became diminished when he laughed at his own witticism.

John Friesen remained noncommittal.

"We're supposed to meet...have a meeting with my father," Chuck explained.

"No, really? A meeting of the ship's officers, and no one told me about it? As the Mayflower's second officer, I better attend."

"That's fine, Chuck. We have other things to do," John broke his silence to diffuse the burgeoning confrontation just as the elevator quivered to a halt and the doors opened. John and Steve departed aft while Stratford and Chuck went right.

As unsettling as the strange encounter was, Stratford sensed there was a deeper truth. The younger Perry held his own impressions about it but had reached the same conclusion.

"Why didn't your dad just pick up a phone and call over the loudspeaker for me?" Stratford asked suddenly. "Why send you to search for me, if it's that important?"

"He said he didn't want anyone to know he was meeting with you."

"Why not?"

"I don't know, Captain. You'll have to ask him." Chuck replied simply.

Charles Perry was standing in the middle of the cavernous landing area when his son and Stratford entered noisily through the heavy steel door.

"David," Charles called loudly, his voice reverberating against the bulkheads. "I was beginning to think you'd abandoned ship."

"Turns out he was in the last place I looked," Chuck said logically.

Stratford suppressed a smile. "That's right, but now that he found me and I'm here, suppose you tell me what this is all about."

Charles addressed his son first. "Chuck, this could take a while. Why don't you carry on with our normal routine?"

Chuck took leave, gratefully, not wishing any involvement in whatever his father intended to share with the Captain.

# Chapter 45

After the younger Perry had gone, Stratford returned to the reason for the meeting. "Okay, then," he said. "What do you want to tell me?"

"Plenty," Charles said dramatically. "But there's something I have to show you first." Mystified, Stratford followed Charles to the storage hangar in which the Olympia was dry-docked. As they went inside and Charles raised the lights, Stratford was once again held in awe by its grandeur. It had been placed in this storage hangar over 16,000 years past. Awaiting a kind of Frankensteinian rebirth, the Olympia had once served the first generation, as it would again the last.

"You remember I led the children on that tour through the Olympia," Charles said in a tone requiring an affirmation.

"Yes, of course. I remember."

"David, let me assure you. Everything was in order, and believe, me, we covered it pretty thoroughly."

"I'm sure you did."

"But look at this," Charles demanded as he pushed aside a jumble of metallic hoses draped over the shuttle. Hanging from the overhead and attached to the Mayflower, they were the shuttle's life source, feeding it the desiccating agents that kept its delicate systems free of corrosion. Charles pointed to a complex piece of hardware oddly out of place where it lay on the floor beneath an open access panel. "See that?" He shone the beam of a small flashlight upon it. "It's a pre-ignition injector; the fuel and oxygen are mixed together and superheated before combustion."

"And without it, the Olympia..."

"Without it," Charles interjected, "the Olympia is just a curious relic from our Earthly past."

Reaching for Charles's flashlight, Stratford walked under the shuttle for a closer look. "It doesn't appear to be damaged," he announced, moving the equipment onto its side.

"I looked at it pretty closely myself. It's intact, alright, and simply needs to be replaced. But there's more than that to consider."

Stratford handed the flashlight back to the electrician. "What's that?"

"The point is, it didn't just fall off. There are four lines that attach to it. That's two in and two out. One or even two could have been loose, but even if you convinced me of that, there's no way all four lines would have been loose enough for it to fall off of its own accord."

The stark realization of what Charles was saying hit Stratford hard.

"There's no question. It had to have been removed," he said soberly, knowing the deeper implications. "That means it was sabotage."

"It's obvious," Charles agreed. "But there's more. Before I sent Chuck to look for you, I'd heard a sound coming from in here, as if something heavy and metallic was hitting the floor. I came in to see what happened, and that's when I sent him to bring you here. I didn't want whoever did this to know we were on it."

"So, you didn't see who did it."

"No, but I know how they got in and out without being seen," Charles said, and placed the beam of his light on a large floor plate under the shuttle. "They had to come in through the service tunnel. That floor plate was up when I got here."

Stratford lifted the heavy steel plate and stepped into the tunnel as Charles handed him the light. "There's a box wrench lying here," Stratford announced excitedly. He squeezed into the narrow tunnel, shining the light beam down its length. Conduits carrying vital fluids encrusted over time ran along the walls next to heavy cables, but Stratford found no other evidence left by the saboteur. "There's nothing else," he announced loudly, his voice hollow-sounding and constricted.

As he extricated himself from the tunnel, he dropped the floor plate into place. "I know who might have done this." Stratford offered warily. He realized that by taking Charles into his confidence, it also placed him in a position of vulnerability. "Woofter," he said simply.

"Woofter?" Charles repeated doubtfully. "You think so? I suppose he's as likely as anyone, but he doesn't appear unhinged enough to do something as purposeless as this. I mean, what would have been accomplished, even if he succeeded?"

"Maybe it's a retribution of sorts."

Charles considered that for a moment. "Why? For what was done to Jamie? If that was true, why wouldn't he take his revenge out on you?"

"Because there might be more to it than just revenge." Stratford answered evasively.

Charles allowed him time to elaborate, yet Stratford remained silent. In an anguished moment of doubt, he wondered about his friend. Could Charles be trusted?

"It appears you know more than you're telling," Charles grinned good-naturedly. "And that's okay, David. But let me tell you some things I know. First, there are candidates I'd consider for this sort of thing before Michael Woofter. Frankly, I haven't heard either Michael or Jamie squawking about what happened. In fact, Jamie seems to have pretty much accepted her pregnancy and is back working her shifts again."

"I've heard that too."

"There's been a lot of negative talk going around. Things you haven't heard, and most of it is directed at you."

"Because of…about Jamie's procedure?"

"Yes. I doubt anyone has said anything about it to your face, but the ship is pretty well divided over it."

"Divided? How do you mean?"

"There are those who agree with what you did, and those who disagree," Charles said, then grinned broadly. "Just for the record, so you know where I stand. I'm one of those who agrees."

"I appreciate that," Stratford said gratefully. "It's nice to know who your friends are, but I did what I felt had to be done for the good of the whole ship. So, yes, I approved it, based on Audrey's recommendation, but Dr. Phen performed it."

"I understand, believe me. That isn't the half of it. Some people are comparing what was done…pardon me for saying…to rape."

Stratford recalled that scene in *Rosemary's Baby*. It was hardly like that.

"A rape by technology, perhaps," Charles continued. "But forced insemination, nonetheless."

"Who's calling it a rape?" Stratford demanded angrily.

"Steve Lester seems to be the loudest critic, I guess. I've heard him."

"Lester, huh? That makes sense." Stratford exclaimed as he recalled the strange confrontation on the elevator. He apprised Charles of the event.

"There you are, David. He'd be my pick to have done something stupid like this," Charles asserted.

"But why would Lester take what happened to Jamie so personally?" Stratford speculated aloud.

"Gallantry, maybe?" Charles joked.

"I doubt it," Stratford said wryly. "Even so, why do something like this?"

Charles shrugged. "I don't know. Maybe he figures it takes the heat off Audrey because there's been as much blame thrown at her and Dr. Phen as well."

Stratford grew darkly serious. "We didn't catch Lester…or whoever did this, but we will have to be wary. There's a saboteur in our midst, Charles, and we have to act under the assumption he'll strike again. Let's go to the control room. There's something I want to show you."

As they were leaving the hangar, Charles had an idea. "I suppose I'd better come back later to re-install that injector on the Olympia."

"You better put the hangar in total lock down too," Stratford advised. "Also, figure out a way to secure the service tunnel."

"Yeah, good point. I guess I could weld a couple loops to the floor plate and then slide a steel bar through. That should hold it."

"That's fine, Charles," Stratford said distantly. He had been looking around the hangar, taking in its immense size but mainly trying to orient himself. "I was thinking: these service tunnels run everywhere, don't they? Do you know where this one leads?"

Charles thought a moment. Then, he turned and pointed dramatically toward the wall behind the Olympia. "The garden is on the other side of that bulkhead."

# Chapter 46

Harmon had been watching Michael perform his duties. He noticed how detached he'd become lately, and the stiff, mechanical way he moved. This from a man for whom his work had always been one of his life's passions. Now, it was merely a vexing obligation.

Harmon well knew, as did the entire ship's company, about the forced pregnancy ordered on Jamie. While his sympathies were with his son and daughter-in-law, he also privately hoped it would give them cause to reflect upon, and reorder, their priorities.

The impending birth of their child seemed to have the desired effect on Jamie, but not so with Michael. His behavior had grown ever more erratic, it seemed, since Jamie discovered that accursed disk. Harmon had resolutely refused Michael's insistence that he watch it. Yet, despite himself, he wondered at the power it must contain, even as he was by instinct repulsed by the damage it caused his family. He felt the depth of his son's despair but could do nothing to lessen it.

The elder gardener had been occupied transplanting seedlings while nearby, Michael prepared a fertilizer/water mixture. Harmon glanced up when he noticed the crop platform directly in front of his son begin to move. Michael had set the system in motion. It moved jerkily at first. Then, it shook and groaned as it gained momentum, rotating the plants through their feeding cycle.

Michael stood eerily still, watching the platform as if hypnotized by its motion.

Harmon left his work and walked up behind Michael. "Hey, are you okay, Son?" he asked loudly.

Michael appeared startled but recovered quickly once his thoughts reconnected with his surroundings. "Oh, sure, Dad," he laughed self-consciously. "Why do you ask?"

"Because I'm your father and I know the difference," Harmon answered curtly. He then returned to his labors, knowing Michael's response belied a troubled heart.

What could his father have meant, Michael wondered. Did he know something? Did his own guilt transmute itself onto his features? Did his father know what he'd done?

In truth, he had done nothing. Failing to disable the Olympia, Michael slipped back undetected to the garden in an agitated state. Yet, he was oddly relieved by his failure.

Continuing his work, Michael adjusted the speed of the rotating crop platform and the amount of "rain" the plants were receiving.

In the peaceful tranquility of his garden, he could think clearly now. He realized that grounding the shuttle would leave him as culpable as the Project's ancestral founders. He saw them as those who had denied their descendants an Earthly paradise. Had Michael succeeded, he could have forced the Mayflower's return to Earth, but in both instances, something fundamental would be denied: choice. Without the shuttle, the Mayflower could not affect a landing. Once the mother ship approached Earth, a signal of distress could be sent and an evacuation arranged to remove and rescue the last generation from the Mayflower.

His and Jamie's attempted abdication from the Project was precluded by the child she now carried. The Mayflower Project, the Mayflower and its ongoing generations were as one, Michael realized. Stratford had been right about that. Had he succeeded in grounding the Olympia, would his selfish malevolence be any less than that of their ancestral fathers?

*If the others could only experience what he had seen,* he thought...

# Chapter 47

Stratford led Charles to the control room and was relieved to find it empty. They could proceed undisturbed. He sat at the control console and began entering commands into the Mayflower's master computer, while Charles sat next to him and looked on.

Charles's interest diminished quickly. "What are we looking for, David?" he said testily, tapping his index finger on the edge of the console.

Stratford hedged answering till he produced results. "This is it," he said and looked up at the overhead monitor. "The Constitution."

As first officer, a thorough knowledge of the document was part of Charles's training, although he could not recall a practical application for normal duties. "What about it?" Charles asked, maintaining a state of denial.

Stratford scrolled down. "Article 5," he said quietly.

Charles knew what that meant. "I guess you think it's come to that?"

Stratford looked skeptically at his first officer. "Don't you?" he asked, incredulous that Charles could ignore what he had seen with his own eyes. "That job that was done on the Olympia? What would you call it?"

Charles nodded reluctantly.

"Look at this," Stratford instructed. For Charles, it felt like an order.

*Article 5: Sabotage and Mutiny*
*...defined as willful misconduct that would result in the subjugation of the majority, with the intended purpose of the disruption of the Mayflower Project and its goals as set forth in Article I.*
Stratford scrolled down further:
*...regardless of an obvious motive, the disruption of machine or man shall constitute sabotage in the first case and mutiny in the second.*

"That's powerful stuff," Charles said, knowing what it implied.

"There's more," Stratford pointed out.

*...the highest-ranking officer, ascribing to the Mayflower Project's stated purpose as described in Article I shall act in accordance with the majority interest, employing deadly force if necessary...*

"It's...that's too real for me," Charles said weakly as he slumped back in his chair. "I know what it says, but it's too real."

Deadly force. The words roiled around in his gut, leaving him in a damp, icy sweat.

Suddenly, the overhead display of the Constitution was interrupted by a strange distortion of colors. Both Stratford and Charles assumed at first it was some sort of technical failure, but as they watched, the picture grew ever more sharply focused.

Stratford stood quickly, angered when he realized what this was. "That son of a bitch," he shouted. Somehow, Michael had transmitted the contents of that disk onto the control room's monitor. Was it appearing elsewhere, too?

A vaguely familiar voice accompanied the action:

*...through hybridizing, you will produce specimens of superior quality...*

Stratford glanced inquiringly at Charles, unsure how this might be affecting him. Predictably, his face registered confusion, but also wonderment at the spectacle. It was Stratford's outburst that caused Charles to rightly assume Michael Woofter was somehow behind this.

"What place could that be?" Charles said out loud, as if airing his thoughts.

Strangely, the sequence began to play again:

*...through hybridizing, you will produce specimens of superior quality...*

"It's Earth," Stratford provided the obvious answer. "Our ancestors' Earth."

"But how could it be possible..." Charles began.

Drawing a substantial breath, Stratford prepared to tell Charles of Jamie's discovery.

"This was the reason...they refused to conceive?"

"Yes, and Michael's attempt to sabotage the Olympia," Stratford said grimly and looked again at the hated images. "And now it's come to this."

Charles understood. "Mutiny," he said simply.

Stratford didn't answer. That one word sent him into a rage as he tried desperately to stop the display, using all manner of combinations of buttons. The monitor responded by playing the sequence, almost in defiance yet again.

"It's beautiful," Charles said reverently. "All those things we've believed about Earth can't be true, then. This proves..."

"Nothing is proved," Stratford broke in angrily. "And that's enough. I won't hear any more along those lines..."

# Chapter 48

Before Stratford could finish, he became distracted by the opening of the control room door, admitting John Morrison. Even before speaking, John looked directly at the monitor. Stratford sighted along the same visual trajectory, realizing even before he spoke why John was there.

"Damn thing must be everywhere," John said breathlessly. "I don't know what that is, Captain, but I can tell you I had nothing to do with it."

"I...we already know, John," Stratford assured him. "Michael Woofter is responsible."

"He is? Then, maybe you can explain what it is, and how he came by it. Because I don't have anything...there's nothing like that in the ship's library."

Charles looked to Stratford for confirmation, then briefly explained the source of the video and the insidious corruption it brought upon the gardener and his wife.

"It all makes sense now," John affirmed when Charles finished. "I can guess how he pulled it off. And maybe I should also tell you, it's probably my fault. I once showed him some basic functions of the studio's equipment."

"Then he could have programmed it to play over the entire ship," Charles reasoned.

"Yes, exactly," John confirmed. He looked away dreamily through the crystal canopy, taking in the vastness of time and space that lie before the Mayflower and its children. "But for what possible gain?" he asked.

*...through hybridizing, you will produce specimens of superior quality...*

"Simple. To try and force the rest of us to his point of view," Stratford responded.

"What view is that?"

"To put an end to the Mayflower Project," Stratford said with high conviction. "First, they tried rejecting it outright by refusing to bear a child. Then, Charles discovered an attempt to sabotage the Olympia…"

"Michael did it?" John interrupted excitedly. "Are you sure?"

Charles explained the details of his discovery. "There's no doubt as far as we're concerned."

"Why do something like that? I mean – what could he hope to gain?"

"The failure of the Mayflower Project," Stratford said dramatically.

John remained unconvinced. "But for what possible gain?" he persisted.

"Michael reached the absurd conclusion that the Mayflower Project should never have taken place, despite the scientific contributions and sacrifices of our ancestors, or even our own," Stratford lectured pedantically but was met with John's blank expression. "Look, it's simple, John," he continued. "Without the Olympia, there would be only one alternative: to turn the Mayflower back to Earth, and in Michael's way of thinking, he'd…"

"What would be gained by that?" John protested.

"Nothing but it puts his descendants back on Earth," Charles rightly observed. "Ours too, I guess."

All three men then fell silent as the monitor yet again displayed the ancient orchard from Earth. Stratford and Charles watched while John began to feel its sway. "Why force us to see this over and over?" he wondered aloud.

"To persuade," Stratford said briskly. "But it's mutiny."

"Mutiny," Charles repeated.

"John, is there any way you can stop it?"

"Sure, I can. It's a matter of finding the source, though, which could take a while. I'm certain he downloaded the disk to a file in the Mayflower's computer because I was in the studio the whole time just before it started playing. Don't worry, Captain," John grinned confidently. "I'm on it," he vowed as he departed the control room.

*…through hybridizing, you will produce specimens of superior quality…*

Charles turned and looked inquiringly toward Stratford as he stepped to the rear of the control room. "Okay. So, what now, David?" he called after him. "Do we just wait?"

Wordlessly, Stratford stood before a large door secured with a time-lock not unlike the garden's vault. "No, we don't wait," he said finally.

Charles watched as Stratford placed first his left palm, then his right against a sensitized plate that quickly scanned each hand in turn with a bright passing light.

Stratford beckoned Charles to stand close. "This is a manual override to the time-lock," he explained. "It requires two sets of scans."

"Really?" Charles marveled. "How is it you know…"

"I've always known," Stratford anticipated Charles's question. "I was shown this room a long time ago. By my father."

"What exactly is in here?" Charles demanded.

Stratford endeavored to demonstrate to Charles the scanning sequence. "It contains the Mayflower's arsenal," he said quietly. He then entered a short series of numbers on the entry pad. The lock disengaged with a loud metallic snap.

"Arsenal?" Charles asked, but realized the meaning of the word, and its consequences, even as he said it: weapons.

Stratford pulled the heavy door effortlessly and activated the overhead lights as he led Charles into the cavernous vault.

Charles took in the vast display of weaponry enclosed in glass cases along both walls. "Do you really believe this is necessary?"

"Sabotage…sabotage and mutiny," Stratford said, reminding Charles of the contents to Article 5. "So, you tell me."

"You believe it's come to his, then?" Charles asked. "You intend to kill him?"

Stratford grew suddenly impatient with Charles's show of pacifism. "Maybe, he'll kill himself and save us a lot of trouble," he responded sarcastically. "But I wouldn't count on it."

At least Charles knew the score, now. For the sake of order, he also knew Stratford was right.

Nevertheless, he sought to distance himself from Stratford, physically and philosophically, by taking in the length and breadth of the vault. Each encasement contained dozens of the particular weapons that were described on plaques. There were $5.56 \times 45$ mm AR15s, FN-FALs in 7.62 NATO, Beretta and Browning semi-automatic pistols chambered in 9 mm.

"Rifle, Winchester, caliber 0.375 H and H magnum," Stratford recited aloud from the case opposite where Charles stood.

"I always wondered what was in this room," Charles confessed, fascinated by the array of weapons. He looked over at Stratford. "But I guess you've always known."

"The WSO was pretty thorough. They wanted us prepared for anything." Stratford observed without any further explanation.

The encasements contained a purplish gas that was a mixture of argon and xenon which served as a preservative for the gun's metal parts and the ammunition. Stratford effected the evacuation of the gas with the push of a button to one case giving rise to a low volume rushing sound.

He opened the case and reached inside. "Beretta, 9 mm," he said, removing one pistol for himself and handed a second to Charles. Holding it close for inspection, he remarked, "Looks pretty good for 16,000 and some years old."

"What am I supposed to do with this?" Charles protested nervously.

Stratford shoved an ammunition clip to place in his Beretta. "Loaded," he said sharply, looking Charles in the eye. Holding the gun sideways for Charles's benefit, he pulled back on the slide and released it, placing a round in the chamber. "Charged." He then pushed the safety to the "on" position with his thumb. "Charged and safe."

Stretching his arm at length, Stratford sighted the tip of the weapon on the point of red light that appeared on the far wall of the vault. "Aim. Then squeeze the trigger."

# Chapter 49

Harmon barely cast a glance away from his workstation when Captain Stratford and Charles Perry entered the office inquiring of Michael's whereabouts. He didn't need to. He'd expected Stratford from the outset after the monitor began its display. By fatherly intuition, as much by instinct, he knew what this was and who was responsible.

As the footage repeated itself, he watched each time with a growing morbid fascination. He realized it was being transmitted throughout the entire ship when a steady procession began arriving at the office by ones and twos. At least half the ship's company had soon made their way here, each seeking enlightenment about this otherworldly paradise. Harmon could offer them nothing, being as repulsed by his son's act of defiance as Stratford. Resignedly, he sent them into the garden, Michael's inherited domain, to be counseled.

"If you're looking for my son, Captain, you'll find him in there," Harmon said gruffly in answer to Stratford's query, indicating the air-lock door and the garden beyond. "But he's not alone. Half the crew is in there with him."

Stratford was surprised by Harmon's cooperation, even if given reluctantly. He rightly assumed the elder gardener hadn't noticed the Berettas he and Charles carried. It wouldn't have made any difference even if Harmon had noticed.

"He's right, David," Charles exclaimed from the observation window. Over fifty of their fellow travelers were gathered therein. He watched in shocked amazement through the misted glass as Michael stood before the crowd engaged in spirited discourse. While unable to hear what was being said, he saw in their faces a rapturous, beautiful glow and wondered at the power Michael's words conveyed.

Harmon continued. "They've been coming here…ever since that thing started playing."

Stratford didn't bother to respond but stepped into the air-lock. He beckoned for Charles to follow. He watched uneasily as Stratford deliberately clicked the safety on his pistol to the off position, then looked hard at Charles, as if seeking his approval. *If nothing else, he was making one thing pretty clear,* Charles thought to himself. He didn't intend to engage Michael in a debate.

"Here goes," Stratford said in a low voice as he opened the second air-lock door.

Both men stepped into the garden, giving Charles a strange feeling: not quite déjà vu, it reminded him of *The Wizard of Oz*.

"Woofter," Stratford shouted, causing the entire gathering to turn in synchronicity. He quickly stepped in front of Charles, distancing him. With his head lowered slightly in a token gesture of humility, he held his right hand aloft – demonstrating a greater purpose. A higher calling.

Everyone saw the gun.

"I want you to understand," Stratford continued. "I'm acting on the authority of the Mayflower's Constitution," he declared, his voice louder now, to carry above the muffled drone of the onlookers.

Meanwhile, Charles had shifted his attention to the gathered throng. John and Mary Friesen were within its ranks as were the Brecks and the daSilvas. Standing in front with arms folded was Steve Lester. He acknowledged Charles with a brief nod as second officer to first officer; next to him was his wife, Audrey. *It was strange to find her there,* Charles thought. She more or less initiated this whole thing.

By far, though, the strangest presence of all was John Morrison, which at least explained why the footage continued to play. What was it that dissuaded him from his duty and drew him here to the garden with the others? Charles looked up and saw again the same truck rolling across that ancient orchard:

*...through hybridizing, you will produce specimens of superior quality...*

The crowd suddenly opened, and Julie Perry, Charles's wife stepped from its midst and hurried to her husband's side. "Charles, can't you stop this?" she implored in a breathless whisper. "Michael told us the truth behind the Mayflower Project. Can't you do something? David listens to you. He trusts you. Do something before it's too late."

Julie reached down to take his hands and was startled by the cold, metallic presence of the pistol he carried in his left. Reflexively, she pulled back. *Lines were being drawn,* she thought to herself.

Everyone became caught up again in the confrontation as they waited for the next move by either man. Without allowing Michael a chance to respond, Stratford lowered the pistol in a deliberate movement till it pointed directly at the gardener. A droplet of intense light made a target on the side of his face, yet Michael remained still, borne of the belief in his own convictions.

Stratford squeezed the trigger.

The pistol recoiled erratically, producing an orange-red flame from its barrel, followed a nanosecond later by a percussive blast. The sound echoed and repeated, then quickly became dissipated by the tangled depths of the garden.

Michael pivoted backward from the impact of the bullet. A collective gasp arose from the crowd – as much for the shot fired as the fact Michael was obviously hit but still standing. Even Stratford was surprised. While having missed his mark, it was in reality a near miss. The bullet had pierced Michael's right bicep and passed through his arm, striking the bulkhead behind with a bell-like ring.

Michael laid his left hand over the wound, his face stoic, belying the burning pain in his arm. His fingers overflowed with blood as it pumped rhythmically forth, dripping and splattering onto the floor.

"Authority?" Michael laughed sarcastically. "Who gave you this authority? Some people who lived and died 16,000 years ago on planet Earth? Look around and tell me, Captain. Do you see any of those people here?"

Stratford had heard enough. With his face contorted in anger, he brought the pistol up from his side, taking aim on Michael, who could only watch helplessly, frozen in the unfolding moment.

It was Charles's voice that broke the silence and stopped Stratford's hand. "David, put the gun down," he shouted suddenly, causing Stratford to turn. "You can't kill him. Are you going to kill all of us, too?"

*Us?* Stratford thought, shocked by this stance being taken by his first officer – his friend. Incredulous, he realized Charles was aligning himself with Michael.

Charles stared defiantly at Stratford and chambered a round in his Beretta. Just as Stratford had shown him. He pointed the pistol tentatively at his friend, leaving no doubt as to his intent. "You can't undo what's been done by killing Michael," Charles said imploringly. Meanwhile, he gripped the pistol firmly and raised it higher. "Listen to me, David. Drop the gun."

Stratford appeared to be contemplating Charles's demand. His shoulders were sloped as if his resolve had weakened. Suddenly, he turned defiantly and fired at Michael, one, two, three times. The Beretta spat out the spent casings as three bullets struck vital spots on Michaels body. This time, he fell.

Charles reacted reflexively, firing just one shot, striking the Captain in the neck. Wild-eyed, he looked at Charles in stark surprise as he dropped slowly, first to his knees then collapsing forward to the floor.

The crowd stood muted in silence, shocked by what had unfolded. They waited for Charles himself to respond. He walked toward Stratford, standing calmly over him, taking in what he had done. What he had been forced to do.

The gathering began to disperse, separating into two groups. Driven by a primordial and morbid curiosity, half the crowd approached Michael's lifeless body. Others stood with Charles, the new Captain of the Mayflower, to observe their former Captain in death.

An expanding silhouette of blood encircled Stratford's head. Charles was astounded by the amount compared to the fake blood he'd seen in movies. He had to look away.

Harmon approached the scene from the air-lock door. The elder gardener had witnessed both shootings form the observation window, and his deliberate gaze informed Charles he held no animosities. With head bowed, he stopped, equidistant between both bodies, his gesture honoring his son and Captain Stratford.

Albert Breck had stood at Charles's side and was first to break the silence. "What should be done now..." he said quietly, then paused, searching for the appropriate title. "Captain," he concluded finally, acknowledging the line of inheritance.

Charles thought about Stratford's young son, but knew he would be taken care of. "I guess I'll need a first officer," he realized aloud. "Do you want it?"

"Sure," Albert grinned. It was ironic, he thought. While no one quite knew the exact circumstances of the Breck families' disenfranchisement from the position of first officer, this rectified that, too.

"Anything you need from me, then?" Albert asked.

"Someone needs to clean this up." Charles answered impassively, dropping the gun to the floor before walking away.

# Chapter 50

The garden had been Michael's sanctuary. At the conclusion of the double funeral held for Captain Stratford and Michael, Jamie felt herself drawn there to stand in his presence.

Throughout the ceremony, she contained her emotions. She held no bitterness. Not even for Michael's assassin. She even managed to deliver a eulogy in her husband's honor. She quoted from the ancient note preserved in the archives that had been given to the first Captain Stratford at the time of the Mayflower's departure. The President had wished the travelers "success, hoping they would be taking with them only the best of human qualities." Michael had often quoted from this, optimist that he was, believing they had done just that.

As Jamie progressed deeper into the garden, the dark canopy imparted a melancholy that finally broke her resolve into a flood of tears. Stopping, she looked up as droplets of fresh water mixed with her tears and washed them from her cheeks.

Like an echo through time, Jamie pondered the President's words and believed they had indeed brought with them the necessary qualities. *It might have seemed an eternity,* she thought, but she believed they had indeed, after all.

*"Avarice and greed are gonna drive you over the endless sea.*
*They will leave you drifting in the shallows*
*Or drowning in the oceans of history*
*Traveling the world, you're in search of no good.*
*But I'm sure you'll build your*
*Sodom like you knew you would.*
*Using all the good people for your galley slaves.*
*As your little boat struggles through the warning waves,*

*But you don't pay.*
*You will pay tomorrow…*
*Save me, save me from tomorrow."*

**Song Credits**

*Woodstock* by Joni Mitchell

*Space Oddity* by David Bowie

*Surfin' U.S.A.* by Brian Wilson and Chuck Berry

*Expecting to Fly* by Neil Young

*I am the Walrus* by John Lennon and Paul McCartney

*Ship of Fools* by Karl Wallinger

**Film Credit**

*Alien,* released through 20th Century Fox

Printed in the USA
CPSIA information can be obtained
at www.ICGtesting.com
LVHW011709300923
759799LV00044B/888